'A deeply rewarding and beautiful novel . . . Intensely personal, her writing is always spiralling in on itself, towards the condition of myth, and yet it nails the moment, pins down experiences so fleeting that others would never grasp them. What eludes ordinary language, she can capture in the extraordinary argot of her imagination. She wasn't divorced from reality – rather, she had a private glimpse of its heart' Hilary Mantel, *Guardian*

'As an account of what it is like to be an overly sensitive and lonely single woman, it is as true and as piercing as anything I have read in a very long time . . . The novel is exciting for its language – it plays with poetry, magical realism and metaphor in genuinely daring ways – and for the way it embraces themes that will later be central to Frame's best work: the dichotomy between inner and outer worlds, between fantasy and reality, between innocence and experience . . . It is a short novel, but a numinous one' Rachel Cooke, *Observer*

'It is a relief to read this book. The reader knows immediately that the prose can be trusted . . . With absolute assurance, Frame renders the lost, uncertain figure of Grace, and considers perhaps the most profound questions a novel can ask: what a person actually is, what it means to live . . . If it is rather hard to say what *Towards Another Summer* is about, that is because in the end, like all the best novels, it is simply about itself' Laura Thompson, *Daily Telegraph*

'A reminder of why Frame was nominated for the Nobel Prize. Quite simply, she's a stunning writer' *Dominion Post* (New Zealand)

'Hopefully, *Towards Another Summer* will incite an overdue re-evaluation of Frame's compelling and unconventional artistry . . . Frame's courageous genius aligns her with modernist writers such as Virginia Woolf, Gertrude Stein or Katherine Mansfield . . . However, in many ways she is incomparable' *The Australian*

towards another summer
janet frame

COUNTERPOINT
BERKELEY

Library of Congress Cataloging-in-Publication Data

Frame, Janet.
  Towards another summer / Janet Frame.
     p. cm.
  ISBN 978-1-58243-476-6
  1. Women authors—Fiction. 2. Writer's block—Fiction.
3. New Zealanders—England—Fiction. 4. Homesickness—Fiction.
5. Psychological fiction. I. Title.

  PR9639.3.F7T69 2009
  823'.914—dc22

                                      2008050515

Printed in the United States of America

COUNTERPOINT
2117 Fourth Street
Suite D
Berkeley, CA 94710

www.counterpointpress.com

Distributed by Publishers Group West

10 9 8 7 6 5 4 3 2 1

Contents

'. . . and from their haunted bay
The godwits vanish towards another summer.
Everywhere in light and calm the murmuring
Shadow of departure; distance looks our way;
And none knows where he will lie down at night.'

—Charles Brasch, from 'The Islands'

PART ONE

The Weekend

I

When she came to this country her body had stopped growing, her bones had accepted enough Antipodean deposit to
last until her death, her hair that once flamed ginger in the
southern sun was fading and dust-coloured in the new hemisphere, and she was thirty, unmarried except for a few
adulterous months with an American writer (self-styled) who
woke in the morning, said
   —I write best on an empty stomach,
pulled a small piece of paper from his tweed coat hanging on
the end of the double bed, and wrote one line. One line every
day. She too was a writer, self-styled, and it was in between the
second and third parts of her novel 'in progress' that the weekend intruded itself; it stuck in the gullet of her novel; nothing
could move out or in, her book was in danger of becoming a
'foster-child of silence'.
   Therefore she applied literary surgery to free her characters
for their impelled dance or flight; she wrote the story of the
weekend.

It snowed. For weeks the plants in the garden had a shocked
grey look that made you think they'd had a stroke and would
die – the same look was in the face of the old man who collapsed
on the pavement outside Victoria Station, and the ambulance
men wrapped him in a grey blanket, and the crowd said

3

—Is he dead, Can you tell, when their face is grey like that . . .

Soot left fingerprints everywhere; after the first night of glossy snowfilled sleep the city had its way with its own lust of smoke, torn paper and bus tickets. The twelve crocuses in the front garden of her flat softened in their tawny shell and pushed forth limp cream-coloured shoots. The tree by the wall in the corner that had shed its leaves before Christmas, continued mysteriously to release dry crackling skeletons that drifted against the back door and over the drains, covering the small coral reef of rust that spattered at the mouth of the downpipe. In the back yard there were three tubs of plants – two of evergreen trees, evergreen in name only, for their stout leathery leaves were shrouded in soot; and one geranium, its leaves withered, its stalks like tendrils of ageing hair growing from the soot and slush-covered earth. Were the geraniums dead? Every time she looked at them she asked were they dead, for in her own country she had never known geraniums not to be in blossom, they possessed too much fire to let themselves lie dormant, 'banked' during the long winter night with their own death-grey ashes.

In my own country.

She didn't use that phrase as much now as when she had first arrived. Then it was At Home, Back Home, Where I come from . . . It's funny over here, you . . . whereas we always . . . you do this, we do that . . . you . . . we . . . here . . . there . . .

And then there was the matter of the Southern Cross, trying to fit shadowy stars into an already crowded northern sky, pushing out Aldebaran, the Bear, dizzy with trying to replace even the swimming city lights with lonely southern stars, but not being able to reach far enough across the earth to capture them; then giving up, forgetting We, there, us, back home, where I come from, in my country; reminded now

4

by only one or two things – the weather in its climate; the drooping geranium – surely if the geranium died everything would die?

Inside, the electric fires sucked in and blew out the same tired stuffy air; the pedal dustbin in the kitchen was filled with empty soup tins; the bathroom walls glittered with damp moss, the congealed moisture of last week's wet washing.

She sat typing her novel.

End of Part Two.

Part Three, page one, page two, page three, 'they told me you had been to her, and mentioned me to him' . . .

Page four.

Then one morning the *Times* for Mr Burton, the *Director's Journal* for Mr Willow, a letter from Nigeria for Mr and Mrs Mill-Semple, a circular for Grace – Dailies Bureau – are your dailies clean, efficient, punctual? Also for Grace the carefully addressed postcard —Miss Grace Cleave: Do you know the temperature is point one-five degrees warmer in Relham than in London. Come and bask in it! Philip Thirkettle.

Now journeys were not simple matters for Grace; nothing is simple if your mind is a fetch-and-carry wanderer from sliced perilous outer world to secret safe inner world; if when night comes your thought creeps out like a furred animal concealed in the dark, to find, seize, and kill its food and drag it back to the secret house in the secret world, only to discover that the secret world has disappeared or has so enlarged that it's a public nightmare; if then strange beasts walk upside down like flies on the ceiling; crimson wings flap, the curtains fly; a sad man wearing a blue waistcoat with green buttons sits in the centre of the room, crying because he has swallowed the mirror and it hurts and he burps in flashes of glass and light; if crakes move and cry; the world is flipped, unrolled down the vast marble stair; a stained threadbare carpet; the hollow silver dancing shoes, hunting-horns . . .

It's no use saying Freud, Freud. People do, you know. Like squeezing a stale sponge.

Nothing was simple, known, safe, believed, identified. Boundaries were not possible, where nothing finished, shapes encircled, and there was no beginning. A storm raged, and Grace Cleave was standing in the midst of it, one hand pressing her skirt against her knees, the other pressing her dust-coloured fading hair fast against her skull. In these circumstances it needed courage to go among people, even for five or ten minutes. A weekend in Relham with Philip Thirkettle, his wife Anne, her father Reuben, and perhaps – Grace did not know – one or two children – seemed a promise of nightmare. No escape. Two or three days. The problems of what time to get up, go to bed, what to say, where to go, and when, had reached, for Grace, the limits of insolubility: you see, during the night Grace Cleave had changed to a migratory bird.

Oh she could laugh at the fact now, although at first she had been frightened. In the afternoon the announcer reading the weather report before the one o'clock news had said,

—A thaw warning. A slow thaw is spreading, with rain, from the west.

Grace went to the window of the sitting room and looked out and felt in her bones the slow thaw moving from the west, and felt her blood stop, swirl to left, to right, in order to rehearse its warm spring flowing; a porous grey raincloud moved in her head and stayed, soaking her once clear cold precise thoughts, exuding them as ragged links of silver, raindrops of vague mist.

She looked beyond the lights of the car saleroom – European Cars, and the tall flats with their floating staircases, underfloor heating, nine hundred and ninety-nine years' lease, into the dark sky where a small ray of sunlight pushed its way through the dense hedge of cloud and stood, green-sleeved, yellow-capped, in a suddenly-summer lane, shining. Her skin grew warm, she released the skirt held stonily-fast against her knees, moved from the window and flopped, anyhow, legs spread, in the deep easy chair which the agent, checking the inventory of the furniture, had described as part of a 'three-piece suite, cushioned, with floral covers'. And that night Grace didn't continue with page four of the third part of her novel. She went to bed early, carrying a sleeping tablet in a little aluminium foil dish which had held a Lyons' Individual Apple Pie. She took the pill, slept, and woke at midnight, and lay thinking of temperature, light, migratory birds, Coriolis force; and the slow thaw spreading, with rain, from the west; and the misty cloud gathering in her head, and her freely flowing blood released from its glacial well; and her heart beat faster as she felt on the skin of her arms and legs, her breasts and belly, and even on top of her head the tiny prickling beginning of the growth of feathers. She jerked her arm from the bedclothes and plunged the white knob which switched on the bedlamp; she threw back the blankets and examined her skin. No feathers. Only a sensation of down and quill and these, with other manifestations of the other world, could be kept secret; no one else need learn of it. In a way, it was a relief to discover her true identity. For so long she had felt not-human, yet had been unable to move towards an alternative species; now the solution had been found for her; she was a migratory bird; warbler, wagtail, yellowhammer? cuckoo-shrike, bobolink, skua? albatross, orange bishop, godwit?

———

She slept, and woke again when the early morning traffic had begun to flow and the first underground trains shuddered through the earth, they seemed quite near, she wondered if the line were directly beneath her flat, she always meant to ask about it but kept forgetting to locate the regular five-minute shudder. Ah, then she remembered. She knew she had been concentrating on traffic in order to forget her most urgent topic of thought; she had changed to a migratory bird.

How do you feel? she asked herself, no longer afraid, almost enjoying the humour of the situation.

—OK, she replied. Not much different, only relieved that at last I know; but it's going to be lonelier than ever now, there's the thought that once I've established myself as a bird there'll be no stopping me, I might change to another species, I might move on and on – where? I don't know, but farther and farther away from the human world.

She buried her face in her pillow; she tried to find reasons among the coloured lights flashing from the back of her eyes, among the red and yellow stripes, the brown trees, the sun moving in the west corner on the end of a crimson string. Why a migratory bird? No doubt because I've journeyed from the other side of the world. Perhaps I'm homesick for my own country and have not realised it. Am I homesick? I haven't thought of my land for so long; my land and my people, that's how it is spoken, like a prayer, the kind which murmurs I possess rather than I want, an arrangement of congratulation between myself and God; I've tried to forget my land and my people; when the magazines arrive I thrust them unopened at the back of the wardrobe; but I read the letters – Do you remember Willy Flute, you know Willy Flute who used to hang round Mary Macintosh, well he's dead. Willy Flute? With the sunlit eyes? Mary Macintosh? The stuck-up tart in the Post Office at the Motor Licence Counter? No, I don't remember them, I am rocked to sleep, numbed, at least *I'm* not going to write poems and stories which begin *In My Country*, and are filled with nostalgia for 'branches stirring'

'across the moon' – where? At Oamaru, Timaru, Waianakarua?
No, that way of thinking and dreaming is not for me.

I'm a migratory bird. Stork, swallow, nightingale, cuckoo,
shearwater. Sooty shearwater – you remember they live in
burrows, you catch them down south, and they cover your
mouth and face with dark brown grease, it's like eating earth
made into flesh and fat, and afterwards you're so heavy you
seem to sink into a fat-swilled grave, deep, warm as a muttonbird burrow – there, I've said it. Muttonbird. No. Sooty
shearwater. And there's the Maori name *titi*, old Jimmy
Wanaka knew it, he was my father's oldest friend, the first
Maori engine-driver in the country – you remember the week-
ends they fished together for salmon, the time they left their
fish in the engine shed 'out the Waitaki' while they went for
a meal, and the fish was stolen, and mother composed the
inevitable ditty,

> 'One day when Jim and I went up
> to the house for a bite and sup,
> someone stole into the shed
> where we were to lay our bed;
> someone stole our salmon, someone stole our salmon,
> I know 'twas only gammon –'

– there followed a mumbled last line which no one could
understand, the kind of tone used for putting across vulgarity,
except that my mother could never be 'vulgar' . . .

Oh no, I must not remember, Grace thought. I'm a migratory
bird. I live in London. The Southern Cross cuts through my
heart instead of through the sky, and I can't see it or walk
beneath it, and I don't care, I don't care. I no longer milk cows
or sit all day watching a flock of sheep, or walk beneath the

9

bark-stripped gum trees by creeks and waterfalls bedded with golden pebbles; what sparkling air; I've never seen so many leaves, spring, summer, autumn and winter, I'm buried in leaves, see my hand reaching up from their softness, Help.

————

Here – the trembling ever unbroken shell of traffic. Blossoming cars at the wayside. The trap of comparisons as futile as racing to put potatoes in a basket.

Smiling, Grace Cleave got up, washed, dressed, made her bed, and no longer afraid of being a migratory bird she went to the window and looked out again at the slow thaw arriving, with rain, from the west. Then she unbolted the back and front doors, slid the chains from their grooves (burglars! a robbery every night!), unsnipped the Yale snib, released the Chubb lock, and opening the front door she went upstairs to collect the mail.

—Miss Grace Cleave. Do you know the temperature is point one-five degrees warmer in Relham than in London. Come and bask in it. Philip.

2

Grace Cleave, as I've told you, was a writer, although land-
lords with financial fears preferred her to introduce herself as
a 'journalist' or a 'private student' or 'someone engaged in
professional work'. It was those who described themselves as
writers, she learned, who appeared in Court on the charge of
not having paid their rent, fares, bills for meals eaten recklessly in cafes. In a mocking voice the prosecuting counsel
would remark,

—He describes himself as a writer, Sir.

—A writer? Dear me, I thought writers were highly paid
these days. Television, films etc. Why not pull yourself
together young man and try to get into television, write something the public want, don't get mixed up with these fringe
people crusading for peace and poetry, put yourself in a well-
paid job, and then I won't have you before me month after
month for defrauding estate agents, restaurants, British
Railways . . . these offences can lead to something worse . . .
your father was a civil servant, too . . .

A writer collected complications, like the sooty dust that
made an indelible stain on your clothes when you walked
through a paddock of paspalum – that was in Auckland.
Province full of ticking insects, loud-throated birds, warbling,
chirruping, striking bells, the air like polished silver . . .

Being a writer, and returning home tired after every venture, you are so surprised to find on yourself a slowly spreading stain of publisher, critic, agent. You turn in panic to the household hints in *Pears Cyclopaedia*; running your finger down the list of stains – acid, blacklead, blood, candle-grease, green ink, marking ink, Indian ink, nailpolish, nicotine rust scorch sealingwax soot tar whitewash wine, and the remedies – water, turpentine, methylated spirits, carbon tetrachloride, photographic hypo, vinegar. You wonder which stain and which remedy would apply to publisher, agent, critic. Nailpolish? Blood? Wine? Candlegrease? Photographic hypo? Then you realise there's nothing, you can neither identify the stain nor remove it. Feeling resigned, depressed, you set out on your new venture, returning once more through the paddock of paspalum; and the stain spreads.

At the close of her latest venture when she was walking slowly back home, Grace collected an interview with someone from a magazine. Bother. Acetic acid? Photographic hypo? It was no use, there was only the time-proved long-drawn-out remedy that her mother used to adopt, inspiring fury and impatience by her faith in it.

—The air will take it out. Exposure to the air is the best remedy.

But there was so much air, and how could you communicate with it, to tell it to stop by and help, and how did you know which air to address?

———

The man from the magazine came to the flat. From the second armchair of the suite with floral covers he asked Grace questions to which she replied from the first armchair. All was in order. She muttered,

—I've nothing much to say, I can't talk of anything. Influences? Oh let me see, let me see.

Silence.

Philip Thirkettle had the newly-bathed, immersed look of English intellectuals. He gestured readily, he was eager, lively. Grace had put on her blue checked skirt and her blue nylon cardigan with the dipped front and plucked one or two hairs from between her breasts in case they showed when she leaned down, but she needn't have worried. She had been liberal with deodorant too, gritty white neutral-smelling substance in a small pink jar, but again she needn't have worried. It was her mind he wanted to reach, and nobody, by conversation, could ever reach Grace's mind. Like the grave, it was a 'private place', and could not be shared.

Influences?

Oh the usual I suppose.

—How do you go about your work?

—Oh, I, wait a minute, I can't think, I've never been interviewed in my life before, I can't think, I'm senile – do you think I'm going senile?

She made tea. They stood drinking it in the kitchen. She waved towards the refrigerator which throbbed like an incubator surrounded by nursery-coloured walls and 'working surfaces'.

—I'm not used to this. I've just moved in. I've never had a flat of my own before.

He told her about his wife, his father-in-law, the time he had spent in New Zealand.

—New Zealand? Well, I wouldn't know, she said, dismissing the country. —I've been so long away. This is my home now. There's gentleness here.

He insisted. Remember this, remember that.

—I don't remember. I wouldn't know. It wasn't in my time. That was after I left . . .

—Don't you ever want to go back?

Grace smiled thoughtfully, choosing her answer from an uncomplicated store of samples put aside for the purpose.

—I was a certified lunatic in New Zealand. Go back? I was advised to sell hats for my salvation.

A spasm of sympathy crossed Philip's face. Good God, she thought, I've said the wrong thing, the tender mind etc.

—But don't you miss it all, I mean . . . don't you miss it? Don't you prefer it to – this?

—I don't know, I don't know. I miss the rivers of course. Oh yes, I miss the rivers, and the mountain chains. I've never been interviewed before.

—Forget about being interviewed. We're drinking tea.

—I'm sorry. I'm sorry. I've never been interviewed before.

Philip Thirkettle looked embarrassed.

—Don't apologise. Listen, why not come up and stay with us, anytime. You'll like Anne, you'll like Anne's father, he was a sheep-farmer once, you can talk to him about sheep, diseases of sheep, liver fluke, footrot –

—Pulpy kidney, pulpy kidney –

—Do come. Anytime. Why not Christmas?

—Christmas?

—Think about it. Goodbye now.

—Goodbye, Grace said, adding desperately as he went out.

—I've never been interviewed in my life before!

3

A month before Christmas Grace went into hospital, into the wrong zone for her 'residential area', and during her four weeks in hospital she was terrified of being spirited away to a different 'zone' where there would not be as much kindness or understanding. Intermittently, she felt safe. She learned two songs – 'I want to be Bobby's girl' and 'Let's twist again as we did last summer'.

There was much activity – dancing, painting, games. Once Grace played a game of chess with the doctor in one of the side rooms. He had a bald patch as round as a penny on the back of his head. Leaning forward, carefully, deliberately moving his black pawn, he snatched her bishop en passant.

—I'll mate you yet, he said. —I'll mate you.

The room was small and hot. Grace blushed.

She left the hospital, returned to the flat, and spent Christmas reading Samuel Pepys, To My Accounts, and only once or twice she remembered the Thirkettles and the hurried notes they had written.

—So glad you're coming for Christmas. There's a train in the afternoon. Book or you'll have to stand in the corridor. Philip will meet you at the station.

—I've had to go into hospital . . .

—We're sorry about this. Why not come when you've left hospital? You can stay in bed all day if you wish.

—OK. Later then, the end of January, early February.

———

And then, suddenly, between Part Two and Part Three of the new novel, this card, *Come and bask in it*. This card, arriving just when the decision had been made which she had been awaiting for years, ever since she ceased being human, ever since she retired to her private world, although keeping open certain necessary vague lines of fatuous communication with the outside world: she was a migratory bird. Stork, swallow, muttonbird? Godwit?

How could she explain to anyone? How could she go anywhere for the weekend without remarking at some time, in some place, causing everyone to look terrified or sympathetic or embarrassed,

—You know, of course, that I'm not a human being, I'm a migratory bird.

She laughed hysterically when she thought of the situations which might arise.

—There's a possible explanation, her doctor said wisely when she told him. —Are you eating, sleeping? You must eat, you know. Let me put it on record that you must eat.

Sitting at the terrible banquet she thought herself like the comedian in the films who waiting in vain for his food, signalling waiters who ignore him, finally seizes the menu and begins to chew it, then starts on the tablecloth, breaks off a leg of the chair or the table, his hunger can't wait any longer, and what a screaming of laughter from the audience, oh was ever anything so amusing, such eating is so amusing.

—Of course I eat, Grace said coldly.

—Fine, fine. I just wanted to put it on record.

She caught the forty-five bus back to her flat and looked

miserably out of the sitting room window at the pile of dead leaves, packets, papers, bus tickets – there was a man this moment passing the flat. There. Screwing up his bus ticket and throwing it over the low brick wall into the garden. Bus tickets, cigarette packets and papers, chocolate wrappers, all kinds of refuse were thrown into the garden. Sometimes Grace took the hard broom from the coat cupboard in the hall and swept vigorously at the pile of tickets, while people passing (clean, affluent, with leather cases and confident glances) looked astonished, thinking, at the sight of Grace, What a treasure of a daily. When the snow had melted and the shocked plants were revealed in all their ragged lifelessness, impatient for signs of green growth, Grace tugged many of them from the earth. Immediately regretting her impulse, she tried to plant them again although their roots were severed. Against the wall of the Offices of the Examining Board the row of severed plants still stood in brave deceit, and no one would have guessed that the sap in their stems had drained for ever, cut off from the source. Grace gave these plants extra attention. When she entered the flat through the garden she was careful to walk just once or twice beside them, in the hope that her nearness would provide the reassurance necessary for resurrection, but it was no use, she had never been deceived in matters of life and death, she could not hope to deceive the plants she had uprooted. News had to be broken quickly, cleanly; snap; a mound of earth or of special care was no concealment.

4

A certain pleasure was added to Grace's relief at establishing herself as a migratory bird. She found that she understood the characters in her novel. Her words flowed, she was excited, she could *see* everyone and everything. She ticked off the days in her diary and thought, Not many weeks now and I'll be finished my story, then I'll be able to emerge to prowl the streets and sniff the spring air.

It's like this:
    She spoke to herself,
    —Ready. Ah, the cameras wheeled into place, the microphones adjusted. She climbs in, looks back. Regrets? The door is clamped shut. The people of the world retreat. Rejoicing fiercely in her aloneness, she is anything now, nothing human – an egg, a hibernating tortoise, a hazelnut; she will circle the earth, like a marble rolled in the dark mouth of the sky; and ha, she'll soon be in space, she'll address her body, her food, her instruments as dogs, Down there, Down! The whirling floating fragments rasp like tongues against her skin, seize her flesh; everything rises around her, like vomit; it is the day when space, not sea or earth, gives up its dead. She smiles, she murmurs, What ever moored me?, peering at the stars, the pursuing fires, the earth wonderfully cultivated with plant brick stone and not a sign

of moving people, animals, insects, commotions of love. Down, dream, down!

Communication is lost.

A faulty instrument, human error; the private pleasure of the certainty of her death, the public premature mourning for a heroine; on the seas the collection of little boats moving into the area of no recovery to witness the end; flags flying; a regatta; representatives native and foreign.

Her ship explodes, is burned; flash in the sky, stain in the sea; nothing human recovered. The boats disperse, the representatives native and foreign return to make statements, issue bulletins.

Night. The writer emerges from her dream.

—Oh God why have I been deceived? Which world do I inhabit?

Down, dream, down!

5

Every few days the cracked-wheat loaf, ninepence halfpenny, has to be bought; on Fridays the milk bill, seven half pints at fourpence halfpenny, paid; half a dozen eggs a week, half a pound of cheese, the daily newspaper, the literary weekly, the Sunday paper, thud, like a dangerous piece of scaffolding, a plank blown by a high wind out of the sky from a never-completed building – what's it going to be, in the end, you ask. A cathedral, a little house, a railway station, a hangar? It's too high to see the structure, velvet sky sags with fog, the newspaper with its insertion, the insertion within the insertion within the insertion (ah, technicolour!) lies heavily on the foot and heart.

Also, there are visits here and there to consult the stains in their places of origin – the publisher with the soft voice (a bookie giving a quiet tip) and the aura of aftershave lotion; his peony-faced son with the quenched dark eyes; his head reader; editors, editors, the agent worried over his diet and elimination; visits from people, too. The phone rings. Time after time when the phone rings it is Sorry wrong number, but tonight it is Harvey.

—A friend in the States gave me your address. Can I come over tonight, about nine?

Pause.

An American medical student? That *will* be pleasant. Tête-à-tête, sherry, coffee. Do I look like a writer? I should have straight black hair falling over my shoulders; my face should be pimpled and pasty; my shoes should be split at the sides; yet I should look *interesting*. Do I look like anybody, like myself? I wish I knew what to say, I wish I didn't dry up when confronted with people. A slight hope; tonight; sherry; tête-à-tête.

Pause.

—Yes, do come. I'll expect you at nine.

—May I bring my girlfriend?

Pause.

—Do, do.

The old frustrated witch dancing around the cauldron,

> 'and like a rat without a tail,
> in a sieve I'll thither sail,
> I'll do, I'll do and I'll do . . .'

———

Just after nine that evening the doorbell rang and Grace admitted Harvey and his girlfriend Sylvia.

—I'm Harvey.

—I'm Grace.

—I'm Sylvia.

Smiles, everyone established, and while Grace showed them into the sitting room with its floral suite, its lamp standard, desk, reproduction wine tables, electric fire, Chinese prints, Beautiful New Zealand Calendar, postcard of Beethoven ('Celui à qui ma musique se fera comprendre sera délivré de toutes les misères où les autres se traînent'), she thought, These Americans are fitted with a revolving radar tower for picking up women.

She remembered her own American, pleasurably inhabiting her past; their impulsive loving over a period long enough for it to gather rainbow tints, reflections, absorbing sea and sky and almond blossom before it became the usual miraculous bubble-nothing, and she and he, surprised, spread their wet fingers, breathed on them, blew them dry, and there was not a sign anywhere that anyone might know; nothing; only the shadow, the preserved memory; already the acid in which it was embalmed was corroding it; she had hoped that wouldn't happen, but how could she have prevented it? How could she have made love with someone who at the moment of climax began to recite *Gunga Din*? Perhaps that was not so unfortunate – he could have recited lines from *If*, 'If you can keep your head when all about you . . . if you can walk with kings nor lose the common touch . . .'

The common touch.

Although Grace had prepared her information on Klinefelter's Syndrome, it seemed that Harvey was now pursuing a different line of research. His girlfriend lectured in Economics, she said.

He was dark, inarticulate, and looked frail.

Grace poured sherry. The other world intruded. She could say little.

—Nice flat you've got here. Where Sylvia stays there's a skylight in the bathroom and the snow falls on the lavatory seat –

—It's been snowing a long time. Will it ever stop?

—Weeks. Do you know marihuana?

—Who?

—Marihuana.

—I've read somewhere, I've heard, you can grow and harvest it in London. Where I lived in Ibiza –

(Ah, now she would talk to them, she would tell them of the moonlight sharp as flute-music on the cobblestones.)

—Yes I know someone who lived in Ibiza. He's a writer.

—You mean, Sylvia, he *calls* himself a writer. He'd like to stop by and see you sometime.

22

—Oh?

Grace poured another sherry. She could feel a flush spreading over her cheeks, making its centre furnace in two spots on either side of her nose.

—No, I don't smoke.

—You don't? Sylvia doesn't, do you Sylvie?

Sylvie!

—And I don't care for it myself.

Observing them carefully, Grace knew a sudden feeling of superiority. They were young, flowing, so conventionally wanting to be unconventional. There was a small element of hero-worship, too, in their attitude to her, although perhaps it had been stifled by their discovery that she, a writer, lived in a flat which held a three-piece suite with floral covers. They had been disappointed that she hadn't much interest in marihuana. They fitted so neatly into the psychological classification *Post-Adolescence* that Grace began to doubt their ability ever to escape, to struggle through the bleak unfriendly no-man's-land, risking starvation, wounding, death, to the next acceptable age-area prepared for them.

(Feeling for a moment the lonely chilling wind between her shoulder-blades, Grace drew her breath in a quick gasp and shiver.)

They stared at her. She was silent. Dare she lean forward, she wondered, and ask, as one who had escaped,

—Harvey, Sylvia, do you intend to be wedged for ever?

Wedged. What do you mean?

Can you move quite freely where you are? Sure? When you get to no-man's-land you will be able to run, dance, shout, starve, die. Don't you feel cramped?

Immensely superior, free, a member of another generation, Grace refilled the sherry glasses, slopping a little over the edge of the glass-topped table.

—Oh, the carpet!

23

Yes, the carpet. The agent had been careful to state that it was new and of good quality. The carpet, the chairs, the floral covers, the Chinese print above the mantelpiece, the reproduction wine tables . . .

Harvey and Sylvia were talking together. Grace thought, I must try to listen, to concentrate, to make some intelligent remark. After all, I'm a writer, and many writers are intelligent, and didn't I manage quite successfully with those tests at the hospital, matching patterns, fitting blocks together, emptying and filling five and seven pint vessels, striking out words and ideas which did not apply?

—You go to the theatre much?

—No, Grace said quickly. —I'm meaning to, some time. I saw *Macbeth*. Yes, I saw *Macbeth*. Duncan was an old man wandering around in a nightshirt.

—Oh? (Politely.)

Perhaps they're not interested in Shakespeare, Grace thought. They're more interested in the avant garde plays. They do madmen very well on the stage these days. I *know*. But to me, if I consider the matter, the avant garde plays are as much behind the times as Shakespeare.

—More sherry? Oh, sorry, there's no more. Coffee?

Harvey stood up. He had been sitting on the sofa. Grace had been surprised when they sat in different chairs, she had expected them to sit together, to embarrass her with exchanged glances and entwined limbs, but they had separated and established themselves each in a prim attitude on the edge of the sofa and chair. Grace had been disappointed that they did not fit in entirely to her classification . . . didn't everyone know that all Americans . . . all students . . .

Harvey would make a good psychiatrist, although his face had not yet that certain expression which betrays the necessary constipation of feeling.

—It's late, he said. —I have to pack, I'm leaving in the morning.

—Leaving?

Grace was dismayed and alarmed. He should have told me, she thought.

—Oh I'd no idea you were leaving, if you're leaving, well, you must be off –

—Yes, we must be off now, it was nice meeting you, and thanks for the sherry. At Sylvia's place there's –

—Yes, and at Harvey's place there's –

See, already they were exchanging identities, like practised lovers. Grace supposed they had made love. She was pleased at the thought. Ah well, she thought recklessly, a little jealously, How young they start, what a wonderful fleshy confusion it all is, and it's theirs by *right*, oh oh, and my dressing-table is so tidy, hand lotion, talcum powder, and my bed so neat with the candlewick bedspread cleaved beneath the pillow . . .

Going out the door Harvey smiled shyly and drew a brown-paper parcel from inside his coat. He undid the wrapping.

—Will you sign this? Do you mind?

It was her latest published venture. She felt angry and embarrassed.

—Oh dear. I don't like to be faced with it so suddenly. I usually hide them away in a cupboard.

Harvey and Sylvia looked at her. They seemed puzzled and disappointed. A writer not wearing tight black slacks, not having long black hair, living in a smart flat with a three-piece suite with floral covers (*floral covers*) in the sitting room, not smoking marihuana, and now ashamed of her writing.

—You ought to be proud, Harvey said. —This friend of ours who calls himself a writer sat up all night reading your book.

—Did he?

25

She tried to sound enthusiastic. —Did he? That's nice. I'm pleased about that.

She *was* pleased.

She took Harvey's copy of the book.

—What shall I put in it?

—Oh, just your name, you know, compliments from the author, that sort of thing.

Feeling ashamed once more she wrote From Grace Cleave, shut the book quickly, and gave it to him.

—If you're writing to Tom, Harvey said, —give him my regards. He works too hard, you know. We're all worried about him.

She said goodbye, shut the door, locked the Chubb lock, murmured Oh God, Oh God, returned to the sitting room, rearranged the cushions, took the sherry glasses into the kitchen.

Another encounter with people successfully concluded without screams or tears or too much confusion.

I'm doing fine, she said to herself, as if she were one or two days old and had finally mastered the art of breathing.

———

As she lay in bed that night she thought of Tom. 'Poor Tom, poor Tom's acold.' It was he who had given Harvey her address. She and Tom were of the same generation. Harvey had said he was 'worried about Tom' as if Tom were an old man not used to the traffic, not quite right in the head, not knowing what was 'best' for him, in the irritating manner of old men. It was an effort for Grace to think of Tom in this way – to her, at least until a year ago, he was the handsome blond University student who had (miraculously) sat beside her at a lunch-hour music recital, admired her coat (if only he'd known it was the first coat she'd ever had!) and asked

—Are you going to Phyllis Hall on Wednesday?

With her characteristic obtuseness she had replied,

—I've never been there. Where is it?

Tactfully he explained that Phyllis Hall was a pianist, and would Grace like to go with him to the recital.

Grace shivered with delight and said No.

Although her picture of Tom had been brought up to date by his visit to her in London a year ago (tonsils out, ulcer removed, haemorrhoids under control, spectacles fitted, hair thinning) she still thought of him as the romantic young man who played *Isle of the Dead* on the Music Department gramophone, who lectured at the local WEA and caused a sensation by wearing red socks; whom all the men envied because the women swooned over him . . . And now here was one of his research students worried about his long hours of work, his health, his unwillingness or inability to refuse demands to lecture at conferences, his courage in moving at his age to a new line of research.

At his age!

—I've a copy of his book on Dyslexia, Grace had said proudly to Harvey who had replied, fervent with admiration,

—Yes, it takes a lot of courage at his age to venture into new research.

Tom was forty.

—I've learned so much from him, Harvey had said. —How to discipline my working – why almost every evening he doesn't stop until after eleven, and he's first there in the morning . . .

Yet beneath Harvey's admiration and gratitude ran the theme, 'Poor Tom's acold, poor Tom's acold.'

Grace shivered, pinged the knob on the base of the bedlamp, turned her back to the window and her face to the darkness, and closed her eyes. Harvey and Sylvia had said they would visit her again before he returned to the States, but she knew

27

they wouldn't. Grace was used to not being visited. There was always a flurry of it's great to know you, then disappointment that the woman who wrote books had difficulty in speaking one coherent sentence; then silence, silence.

What else could you expect when you were not a human being?

———

The morning after she received the postcard Grace replied Yes, she would visit Relham for the weekend. She plunged her reply into the metal-mouthed lucky dip Posting Box at the Gloucester Road Post Office, and then worried all the way home that her arm was not long enough to reach down, find her letter, tear it to pieces to be thrown over the fence in bold litter-lout fashion, among the huddled sparrow-grey withered plants and brittle dead leaves of Hereford Square garden.

6

The Friday before the weekend another stain unexpectedly marred Grace's progress through her field (she used the word 'field' more than 'paddock') of ventures: there was to be an interview recorded for the Overseas Service of the BBC.

In spite of her protest that she was habitually unable to answer questions about her work, unless they were given to her in advance, the questions were kept secret from her until she arrived at the studio. Half-heartedly, because she did not keep copies of her books, she had borrowed a copy of the latest from a friend, meaning to study it chiefly to find what it was about; she had flipped through the pages, not daring to read them – God what was the use? Then she had thrust her friend's copy in the coat cupboard, on the cardboard tray where she kept the spare parts of the vacuum cleaner, the garden trowel and fork, a blood-stained handkerchief, electric light bulbs. Then she had set out for the BBC.

Too early as usual, she loitered around Charing Cross Station, in the Ladies' Room, reading a crumpled *Daily News* found on one of the seats beside an elderly woman who slept and snored, still clutching her bulging shopping bag. Every time the woman moved in her sleep the movement seemed to entice a current of air to pass through her, and her smell came blowing towards Grace, as from a stirred plantation of sweat.

Behind the door of the waiting room a notice was pasted, You Need Never Be Stranded In London. It gave the address of a hostel in the East End. Grace looked about her at the women in various stages of sleep and dereliction, and thrusting the *Daily News* Heiress Made Ward of Court Chocolate Bid on to the skirt-polished wooden barred-back seat, she went down the gangplank, holding the brass rail, to the underground lavatories, was given change for threepence by a stout white-coated stewardess or wardress who flourishing a duster opened one of the doors marked Vacant, leaned in, polished the seat, and withdrew.

Still too early, Grace left Charing Cross Station and walked into the Strand. She crossed the road and passed New Zealand House. A few people stood staring with the usual February wistfulness at the displayed photographs of sun and sky and sheep; thinking, Shall I emigrate, they say it's a great life out there, the sun, the beach, your own home. Grace felt herself infected by the attentive longing; an impulse surged through her to go to the Emigration Department, enquire, fill in forms. She could see one or two of the spectators swaying with indecision; then they and she turned from the display window New Zealand Land of Sunshine, and walked on through the grey sleety drizzle, the regular mid-morning migration completed through the simplest cheapest most satisfyingly unofficial procedure of dreaming. On impulse Grace retraced her steps for a few minutes. She did not go into New Zealand House. The last time she had gone there to make some enquiry the receptionist had looked haughtily at her,

—Were you thinking of emigrating? Would you like some official literature about New Zealand? You can read up about the country and see whether you might be interested in going there.

Pleased, yet ashamed at not being recognised as a New

Zealander, Grace had said quickly, No thank you, and hurried from the building, glancing about her with a feeling of guilt as she left, letting her gaze rest a moment upon the people sitting in the Reception room reading *New Zealand Air Mail News*. Do I know any of them? she thought. Who are they? Farmers, students, secretaries, lawyers, teachers, doctors? They bore no distinguishing mark. Would they speak to her, saying —You come from New Zealand don't you, North or South? How long have you been over here? When are you going back? What do you think of life over here?

No one spoke to her. Feeling as if she were an intruder, cooperatively taking a pamphlet on Immigration from the table beside the desk, establishing herself as a 'Pommie', she went out to rejoin the stream of people in the Strand, walking slowly towards Bush House. The chalked placards proclaimed *Frizzle – Freezing rain plus drizzle! New word for weather!* It's not often, Grace thought, that the language is made a headline.

———

The producer was crisp, the interviewer efficient. Both had notes; Grace held only a glass of water which she twirled in her hand, answering or not answering the questions, breaking off in midsentence, her mind blank. She sighed, repeated Sorry, Sorry in a whisper, shaking her head.

—I don't know, I don't know. What are my books about? How should I be able to tell? My style? What does it matter?

She wondered whether these accumulated stains that seemed so much a part of her essentially private ventures would in the end spread over most of her life, sink deeper and deeper, be absorbed as a poison which could be removed only if she swallowed a violent medicine which would force her to vomit her whole life – all her treasured experiences and dreams – and be left weak, unable to digest more of life, sitting, cramped with pain and lassitude, in a bed or wheelchair until she died and was buried here, in London, with a representative from New Zealand House taking time off to trim the frayed thread-dropping embarrassments of untidiness woven when a stranger without next of kin dies ten thousand miles from home.

—Miss Cleave, are you trying to put across a message? It has been said, Miss Cleave, that you resemble . . . Could you tell us briefly the *essential* nature of your work . . . Do you think you will ever return to New Zealand?

The interview was finished at last. Humiliated, inarticulate, Grace sat twirling her glass of water. Why couldn't she speak, why couldn't she speak?

The producer came from the recording room, opened the door and looked in.

—I'm sorry, Grace said. —I haven't anything to say, I haven't anything to say.

The producer spoke crisply. She reminded Grace of the manageress of the dairy at the corner of the street near her flat: an efficient woman who knew which part of the refrigerator held the stale, and which the fresh milk, and who each time chose, automatically, the stale milk. There were stale biscuits too, and wrapped cakes and old pies arranged on the counter; the woman was surrounded by an array of yesterday's and last week's food and drink which had to be sold.

—Quite good, the producer said. —We'll make something of it. (This packet of biscuits is specially reduced – would you like to buy some?)

—Yes, quite good. The silences were *so effective*.

Grace ruffled her feathers, flapped her wings wildly, went hysterically out into the Strand, found a cafe where she sat on a tall revolving stool, ate bleached cod fillet with chips like a heap of thin twisted yellow nails, and bread brushed with a damp yellow sponge. Then she caught the bus to St Pancras Station. The freezing drizzle had changed to snow, big flakes too extravagant for city distribution, as big as the pages of a huge diary, a month to an opening, fluttering, drifting, the streets full of people hurrying in panic, fearful of burial. Grace almost ran from the bus and collided with a West Indian man standing calmly being snowed on, with a newspaper spread over his head.

—Snow, he said. —Don't you like it?

Grace was ashamed. Of course she liked it, of course she hadn't lost her feeling of wonder at the sight of snow – then why had she been running from it?

—Yes I like it, oh yes.

She pulled her rainhat closer to her head and hurried towards the station; convincing herself as she ran, It's not real snow, it's only city snow, but when you begin to make such distinctions doesn't it mean that everything is lost?

Grace couldn't bear to lose things; her head was always dizzy with looking for the mislaid, stolen, concealed.

———

At St Pancras Station, after inspecting the notices of arrival and departure and the chalked apologies for delays, Grace performed her usual ritual of waiting. She bought a midday newspaper but discarded it because it was filled with Greyhound News. She went to a lavatory and washed her hands, pressing her foot, as directed, on a lever which set free a spurt of hot air to dry her hands. She said No thank you when the attendant offered 'A wash and brush up, fourpence.' She returned to the Waiting Room, warmed herself by the radiator, then emerging into the stark open station she sat on a wooden seat, watching, listening, and it wasn't soot in her eyes that almost drew tears, it was memories at the sight and sound of the grim blustering grunting panting steam-engines, uttering from time to time their triumphant prolonged Haaaaaa, Haaaaa in a deep exhalation of steam, and releasing from a side valve where their ears would be, had they ears, sudden high-pitched jets and spurts in a white thread of scream. On the platform the people moved through smoke, their silhouettes vague, their bodies merging one with the other, their Scottish voices muffled and smokefilled. When Grace followed the arrow to the enquiries department to make sure of the platform and destination of her train, the clerk leaned over the worn counter and said gloomily, running his finger up and down the smudged column,

—Platform seven, arriving at Relham six-eight pm. Central Station.

He looked accusing.

—But didn't you read the notice outside?

—Oh yes, Grace said. —But I wanted to make sure.

The clerk sighed.

—Yes, they all do, they can't trust it in print, they have to hear it spoken. Illiteracy.

Suddenly afraid that even the clerk was not certain, that after all, trust in the printed word had to begin somewhere – perhaps the clerk was not so sure, that here she was, a migratory bird, standing waiting at St Pancras for the train to Relham, and perhaps there would be no train, or perhaps there would be such a crowd that there'd be no room for her.

—Can I book a seat? she asked urgently.

—What? When the train leaves in half an hour's time? Oh no, oh no, that would be daft. Too late to book.

Slowly Grace walked back to her seat near Platform seven. A young woman sitting near zipped open a briefcase; withdrew a sheaf of papers, took a pencil, and with her pencil poised over the first page she turned towards Grace and smiled.

—I wonder, she began. —That is, would you mind if I asked you a few questions?

34

Without waiting for an answer she ran her pencil beneath question one on the cyclostyled sheet,

—Will you tell me, are you at all aware of the Campaign to sell the New Fellas Cornflakes?

———

The train was crowded with passengers. It didn't seem fair that so many were travelling in such weather. They should have stayed home, Grace thought resentfully, finding a corner seat and rubbing clear her small share of window, settling herself to her usual railway dreaming. Suddenly there was a commotion in the corridor, the door was thrust open, and a man and woman, breathless, clutching luggage, burst in, and sat facing each other, the woman in the seat beside Grace.

Slowly the train began to move.

—We just found out in time, the woman said. —Our carriage would have come off at Derby!

—We didn't know, the man put in. —There was no one to tell us, the train is so crowded we grabbed the first seats we could find. We might have been taken off at Derby!

—Just think, the woman murmured. —To be left behind at Derby!

To them, Derby seemed such a dire fate that Grace looked sympathetic and said, in a suddenly unconvinced tone,

—*This* carriage goes as far as Relham . . . doesn't it?

They assured her that the guard had assured them that it did, and once the fact was settled, the other passengers in the carriage (an open one with tables and dust-smelling crimson upholstery) who had been drawn into the whirl of excitement and uncertainty, withdrew, disengaging themselves one from the other, to preserve what was left of their privacy.

The woman opened a paper bag and took out a pear which she peeled and quartered. She gave one piece to the man and offered one to Grace.

35

—No thank you.

—Come on.

—No thank you, no really, no.

The man looked up from his newspaper.

—Come on, you're the only one not having a piece.

—Oh, all right, thank you very much, that's very kind of you.

Grace ate her slice of pear, rubbed clear the misting window and gazed out at the neverending rubbish dump which was the landscape approaching the Midlands but which, as they travelled further north, was obscured by continual snowfall until at last the train moved in a white translucent landscape, as if they journeyed on the face of the moon.

The other passengers in the carriage, their emotions not having been unexpectedly released by the threat of being 'taken off at Derby', maintained their private silence, but the woman chattered freely to Grace, and when her companion, having overcome the difficulty of the Derby threat and being presented with a new more formidable one of wanting to smoke in a non-smoking carriage, excused himself and went to the end of the corridor to light up his Nelson outside the lavatory, the woman explained to Grace that he was her brother-in-law, a steward on the train, who had that morning travelled, working, to London, and was now returning, in state as it were, to their home in Relham. The fact that he knew the railways by heart made it inexcusable, the woman said, that they had boarded the wrong carriage. She herself had been staying in Devon with her sister; it had been snowing in Devon ever since Christmas.

—You going to Relham too?

Grace made the mistake of adding to the Yes, she was going to Relham, the information that it was her first visit there, it was her first visit to the Industrial North.

The woman looked at her with pity and wonder.

—You won't know your way around then, she said insinu-
atingly.

—Oh no, Grace said.

—Relham's a big place if you don't know your way around.
Here, the woman said, rummaging in one of her shopping
bags and finding a bag of sweets,

—Have a sweet. Go on.

—No thank you, no really.

—Go on, you'll be hungry by the time you get to Relham.

Grace accepted the sweet, rewiped the window-space and
looked out, and the woman, taking her gesture as a sign of
unfamiliarity with the landscape and uncertainty about her
destination, said reassuringly,

—Don't you worry, I'll let you know when we get to
Relham. Here – her voice was full of pity –

—Have another sweet.

—Oh not really, well, all right, thank you.

Later when the woman's brother-in-law returned from his
smoke outside the lavatory the woman informed him in a
loud voice which caused one or two passengers to look their
way,

—She's never been to Relham before! This is her first visit
to Relham!

Branded, Grace blushed, sucked hard at her sweet, and
stared through the window. Snow was still falling; occasionally
street-lights threw a buttery glare upon the new bread-white
snow; at intervals along the railway lines golden-red coke fires
gleamed, throwing Santa-red shadows on the snow, while
upon the carriage windows congealed snowflakes flew and
were trapped like pieces of festive cotton-wool. The world
seemed buried deep in snow and sleep, with pillows and sheets
of snow stacked against the dark sky. Grace leaned her head
against the window, closed her eyes, and slept, and when she
woke, with her cheeks hot, her eyes grinding and heavy with

grit and soot, the woman whispered to her, gathering her luggage in preparation,

—This is it. A few more miles and this is it.

—Oh, Grace said coldly, not caring.

—You'll be all right? the woman asked anxiously, as Grace pulled her bag from the rack.

—Someone's meeting me, Grace replied formally, in the hope of ridding the woman of the St Pancras to Relham myth which she had established and which (from the glances of the other passengers – it's late, if she hasn't been to Relham before she might be lost) was beginning to spread through the compartment.

—Someone's meeting me, Grace said again, in a louder voice.

Oh, she could have wept, why did she always seem not to know where she was going, why did strangers always take upon themselves the responsibility of caring for her, arranging things for her, supervising, guiding? What was it in her appearance and behaviour which caused people to want to explain to her, to talk to her in simple language as if she might not understand?

—Yes, someone's meeting me. It's quite all right, Grace said, meaning once more to sound remote and calm, but at that moment the train jerked, stopped, lurched forward again, and Grace's words emerged in an undignified cry which might have been construed as Help. A stout man who had been sitting back to back with the woman's brother-in-law leapt forward and took Grace's arm.

—Are you hurt?

—I'm all right thank you.

Relieved, the man made his escape, choosing the other end of the carriage. Waiting for someone to open the carriage door, for she could never understand how to manipulate the leather strap that opened the window that allowed access to the door-handle, Grace stood watching the hustling pushing people jabbing with their suitcases where their bodies were ineffective as ramming instruments. At last someone opened the door. Grace climbed down and hurried along the platform, surrendered her ticket, and looked around her, waiting for Philip Thirkettle. Oh God, she thought, I can't survive the weekend, I can't go among people for three whole days, talking to them, sharing meals with them, having to decide when to join them and when to leave them alone, when to go to bed, when to get up. What would they say if they knew I had changed to a migratory bird? I can't face it. What shall I say, how shall I make sentences, link words, subject, verb, predicate, while they are listening? At least, she thought, relieved, there are no children, or Philip hasn't mentioned them. Children can be so confusingly direct; they stare, how they stare! At that moment it seemed to Grace that the most frightening thing in the world was a child standing, not speaking, staring at her, staring accusingly, knowingly, pityingly, mockingly, with an understanding which, as a child, he had not yet limited or quelled or destroyed.

In her mind, from the slight information given by Philip, Grace had sketched the Thirkettle 'pattern'. Husband, wife, father-in-law. Philip unable to spend much time with his wife while his wife's attention was turned too often to the care of her father, the former sheep-farmer, miserable, nostalgic, gazing from the windows at the North of England chimney pots instead of at Antipodean sheep and sky and mountains. In an attempt to prepare for the events of the weekend Grace had imagined herself arriving –

—You'll have a drink? Sherry?

Anne beautiful, sophisticated, educated at one of New Zealand's 'private' schools where, Grace remembered with the truth of persecutory desires, all the pupils were 'snobs who spoke haw-haw English' . . . The father-in-law sitting mournfully in a chair by the fire, dreaming of the Canterbury plains and the Nor'wester 'nosing among the pines'. Philip, frustrated, jealous of his father-in-law, wanting to be alone with his wife . . .

—Yes, I'll have a sherry.

Grace's conversation was witty and sparkling, intelligent, memorable; they flushed with pleasure at the beauty of her sentences; her ideas (so original, clearly expressed, profound) excited them so much that they confessed that after her first night spent with them they had lain awake talking, philosophising in a frenzy of imagination.

—Yes, I'll have a sherry.

Considered thus, the fearful prospect of the weekend receded. Why, there was Grace talking enthusiastically about liver fluke, footrot, pulpy kidney, while Philip and Anne, happily alone for the first time in years . . .

As Grace thought of her unselfishness and kindness it seemed that she was not on Relham Central Station but on a cherished allegorical beach, out of danger from all tidal-waves of apprehension, standing, being gently sprayed with 'goodness'; cool and comfortable in spite of the burning sun.

When the weekend was over, the Thirkettles would be grateful to her; she would have brought Philip and Anne renewed happiness.

—Come again, they would cry. —Do come again!

And Grace, used to compromise, glowing with the success of righteousness, that second-best spear in the thrust of love, would feel moderate happiness, promise to 'come again', say goodbye, and finding her corner seat in the train stare mournfully out of the window with her eyes filled with tears and soot.

7

Dried words like drops of blood surrounded her on the platform. Who had spilt them? As far as she knew, no arrow or shot had pierced her feathered breast, and the soaring station roof protected her from wounds made by the sky. She took her handkerchief and rubbed fiercely at the gritty surface surrounding her, then she crumpled her handkerchief, tucked it inside her sleeve, and walked carefully one or two paces, swaying, breathless, unable to escape. There was still time to return to London to the flat, to withdraw in merciful solitude, to sit at her typewriter sending out noisy signals to herself, which was her style and intention in writing. Part Three of her novel waited in its Boa File ('grips like the coils of a Boa'). There was the routine of her working which she used to gain power over her daydreaming. As a last resort there was a sleeping-pill, a tiny white full-stop tasting like poisoned schoolroom chalk. The door to the other world stood wide open. The contents spilled on to Relham Station. Feverishly Grace sank to her knees and began to scrape at litter.

—Lost something? I'll get a cab.

There was Philip, duffel-coated, taller than she remembered him; his hair was yellow, like tussock at the edge of the sea; his eyes were the same colour, darker perhaps, flecked with brown driftwood.

He took her bag.

—Did you find what you've lost?

—Who does? she said neatly, pleased.

They stood in the queue and after ten minutes' waiting they were in the taxi heading for Holly Road, Winchley, ten miles out of Relham.

—A good journey?

—Yes thank you.

—What do you think of St Pancras Station?

—All right, thank you.

—Did you have to wait long?

—Oh yes, Grace said excitedly, proud to be able to communicate some details about herself. —Oh yes, I *always* have to wait a long time. I'm constitutionally *early*; hours and hours early. I don't think I've ever missed a train in my life!

Her eyes were shining, her face was flushed. Oh how wonderful to possess an identifying characteristic! Late, early, tidy, untidy, I'm fearfully slow, I'm always ready on time, I'm so good with children . . .

Children? What was Philip saying about children?

—Anne's the opposite, she's never early. It's a case of rushing to the train, bundling in the kids, leaping on board, slamming the door . . .

Kids?

Philip turned to her suddenly, laughing gaily.

—I don't suppose you mind, having a couple of kids swarming around?

—Oh no, Oh no!

Grace wondered if her heart hadn't sunk through the floor of the taxi. There's still time, she thought wildly, there's still time to escape: children, staring, mocking, pitying, understanding – that was worst – understanding; they would know everything; perhaps they would come up to her and say, What is the pineal gland? Describe your flight feathers. Define Coriolis force.

Trying to calm her mounting panic Grace said bravely,

—How old are your children?

As she spoke she knew that she was not only afraid of the children, but she was jealous of Anne for sharing the repetition of someone as exclusive as Philip.

—Sarah's two and a half, Noel's fourteen months.

Not dangerous ages, Grace thought, with relief. They could be worse.

Yet she felt like weeping. Why hadn't Philip told her about the children? She remembered the times she had said to herself, after her first meeting with Philip, Of course they haven't any children. Of course. Saying it with nasty satisfaction, feeling safe because it was so, constructing a strange imagination of herself as a lost piece of jigsaw that would fit in to the Thirkettle pattern.

—You'll miss Dad, Philip was saying. —He's up in Edinburgh for a three-week holiday.

—Oh I'm sorry, I wanted to meet him.

So there'll be no escape, Grace thought, through talking about liver fluke, footrot, pulpy kidney. She almost sobbed. She wished she hadn't come to Relham, she wished she were back in her London flat listening to the weather report and the news, then switching it off, retreating to the corner by the bookshelf where she had placed her typewriter and parts one and two of her novel in their Boa File. And there would be the Standard Lamp shining its pale white light directly over the keys of the Olivetti; and the rows of books on their shelves on the left, buttressing her against intrusive influences from the Examining Board – she did not know what they examined, or when, or why, but beneath the sound of the traffic outside Grace could hear next door the subterranean murmurous examining, interrupted from time to time by a thumping, shifting sound, as if new standards were being set.

———

You came to me; you said
last night I looked at my hand, and my hand was
     burned,
I have watched the fire spread.
I can do nothing that anyone might envy or put out
     with a terrified foot.
I have watched the fire spread;
now my bones are placed in position, are set,
like the standards you talk of, the murmurous
     examining
by rain probing, the falsely sentimental
snow saying It is not possible
(snowflakes as Get-Well cards, flushed birthday roses,
satin concealment
slipped between my flesh and bone to jolly out
one more responsive year).

Dear mother, dear father dear husband dear child,
there is no answer,
this microphone like a beehive celled with honey
is blocked forever with the sweetness of death.

Since you came to me last night,
and said
what you said
I rode on a red bus
inside a clot of blood
I rode in grief over London,
I smashed nothing, no mirrors, windows, or glass sheets
     of sky.
I prayed Let the world have wonder enough to care
when poets live
and to grieve when they die.

—Four thousand pound houses.

—Three thousand pound houses.

—Two thousand pound houses.

—Just under two thousand pound houses. Here we are.

The suburbs of Relham were replaced by the town of Winchley, and here was the Thirkettles' house almost at the end of Holly Road, on the edge of the moor. The trees were naked ragged sticks with ribbed ice heaped about their roots, and the dark street shone with mirrors of ice obscured by dark blots of snow. Alone among the other houses in the street the Thirkettles' house bore no name; not the Nook, Rydal Mount, Dell Lane, Coral Cottage; merely number five – semi-detached, old, heavy, comfortable, with its other half in silence and darkness like a sleeping limb.

Philip rattled at the chained door.

—This is Anne's doing, he said.

Footsteps. The chain was withdrawn. The door opened.

—This is Anne.

Anne was rosycheeked, almost buxom, certainly beautiful, although (Grace noted with pleasure) she had a double chin. She was followed to the door by a sudden swirl of white like tiny moving candle-flames and Sarah and Noel, stumbling, guttering, arrived to cling to their mother's skirt, to welcome their father and stare curiously at Grace.

—Grace-Cleave's come to stay, Sarah whispered knowingly.

Grace smiled a prim smile. She was terrified they might want to embrace her but they stayed clinging to their mother as she led them along the passage into the kitchen while Philip and Grace followed. Grace tripped over toys and books and blocks. Anne laughed.

—Someone had a throwing session today.

She spoke with a strong New Zealand accent.

45

The room was big, untidy, with shelves in one corner filled with provisions as if the family expected to be marooned for months. Children's clothes, toys, kitchen equipment, news-papers, were slung and bundled here and there in a marvellous conglomeration. Grace looked mournfully at what, to her, seemed the scattered evidence of a house full of love; she was remembering her own home as a child, where the rooms had been a muddle of possessions and furniture and food and chamberpots, and how the man from the 'Welfare' who came one day to inspect the house, following complaints from the neighbours, had not enough perception to discern the roots of love in the wild untidy blossoming; nor, Grace remembered, had their father; nor had the tidy powdered relatives who came for holidays, sleeping in the front room, in a bed with sheets with a vase of dahlias on the dressing-table, sitting on the edge of the kitchen chairs,

—Oh no Lottie, oh yes Lottie,
looking with horror at the muddled kitchen.

—Tidy the place up, the 'Welfare' man had said sternly.

—And have all these dogs put to sleep!

(He meant the stray spaniels who kept having puppies because there was so much new tar on the road that when the dogs went outside they stuck to other dogs.)

—Can't you keep the place clean? their father had said to their mother who, shame-faced, replied,

—Oh Curly it's the best I can do.

Meanwhile the relatives returning from their holidays had spread the news through the Northern, the Southern, and even the Australian branches of the family that 'Lottie was a hopelessly bad manager'.

Staring solemnly the two children flickered around Grace. They wore long white nighties with ragged edges; honey-coloured snot dribbled from their noses, and now and again

46

Anne reached to a roll of blue toilet paper on the mantelpiece, tore a square, and wiped their noses. Grace could not keep her eyes from Sarah and Noel. How beautiful they were! They were waifs with pointed ears and their father's amber eyes; they were like beggars' children. Anne explained to Grace that they had stayed up to see 'Grace-Cleave' arrive, and now they must go to bed. She surged them towards the door; they whimpered their protest. Grace stared at them, her eyes shining.

—Do you know, she whispered, —these children are like little illustrations for *The Borrowers*.

—I'm not a 'stration, Sarah protested.

Philip and Anne exchanged glances which Grace could not read and which embarrassed her – had she said something out of place, perhaps the Thirkettles objected to remarks about their children but they were forced to tolerate visitors who couldn't be expected to understand the plans of intelligent parents?

Suddenly Noel wanted to be kissed goodnight. He moved towards Grace, half-crawling, half-walking, muttering in Martian language, which Anne translated.

—He wants to kiss you goodnight.

Grace kissed him, her face burning.

—I'm quite used to children, she said defensively, adding with reckless inaccuracy, —I used to look after children this age.

Now Sarah, evading her mother's grasp, ran to Grace pleading, —Let me climb on your knee!

Timidly Grace looked at Philip and Anne. Anne nodded.

—Yes, you can climb on Grace's knee.

Awkwardly Grace lifted Sarah who bounced restlessly once or twice, then complained,

—You've got no knee. Grace-Cleave's got no knee.

Grace blushed with shame at her deficiency.

47

Indignant, Sarah slipped from Grace's arms, went towards Anne and clasped her skirt, hiding her face in it, and then, rubbing her eyes, she was suddenly almost asleep. Moving her gently before her, carrying Noel with a practised encircling arm, Anne went upstairs to put them to bed.

—I'll show you your room, Philip said as they went out.

—And I'll show you the study at the top of the house.

Tired and confused Grace followed him.

—

She stood alone in the centre of the room, noting its particulars. Philip had explained that it was less Spartan than the room where she would have slept if 'Dad' hadn't been away in Edinburgh. This was 'Dad's room'. Rush matting on the floor, a comfortable single bed; one or two pieces of heavy polished furniture; a tray of seed potatoes on the sideboard; two or three shelves of books – bagpipe music; *The First War Rifle Brigade*; Lord Montgomery's *Memoirs*; poems by Robert Burns; the Authorised and New versions of the *Bible*; stories by Sapper. Framed photographs of New Zealand scenes were hung on the wall, and over the fireplace a large map of New Zealand – blue seas, green plains, white-capped mountains. Grace reached up and ran her finger around the coastline tracing the once-familiar towns between Oamaru and Dunedin and farther south, pausing at each one to try to capture a memory of it. Maheno: there was a picnic spot near the river – The Willows – where girls from School used to go for their Saturday bike-rides, and the boys and girls for their Bible-Class picnics; where lovers used to bathe naked in the earth-tasting beerbrown swimming hole. Maheno, where the Limited Expresses from North and South used to pass, near Waianakarua,

'Tall where trains draw up to rest . . .'

48

a plantation of gum trees crackling smooth grey flames of leaf, shaking blue dusty smoke as the wind touched them; the rust-coloured engine-sheds; cabbage trees, tussock, swamps, sheep – with her finger on the map Grace catalogued the physical details of the land. She was in the train travelling from Oamaru to Dunedin – why did it seem such a tiny train yet why did the black canopy shrouding the platform between carriages seem of such shiveringly-fearful importance? The usual slow train that stopped at every station to unload and load or merely to loiter and which travelled seventy-eight miles in seven or eight hours did not possess these luxurious black canopies which enabled you to pass, hidden, from carriage to carriage. If you wanted to move along the slow train you had to risk the rush of air on the unsheltered platform, you were jolted, blown on, rained on, and never had there been such a noise in your ears, so much soot in your eyes.

Grace looked about her at the sweaty redfaced passengers whose possession of the train, beginning for most of them when they had left the Cook Strait Ferry at Lyttelton, seemed to provide them with so much influence and power, they stared with disdain at the scattered few boarding at Oamaru, the Refreshment Stop; cream buns and fizz. Then Grace looked out at the sea, the cliffs, the hooded wayside stations Waitati, Puketeraki, Mihiwaka . . .

She drew her finger quickly from the map. No, she would not travel in the Limited from Oamaru to Dunedin.

She stayed in the room. The colours of the map were such delicate pastel shades, as if agriculture were a cosmetic. There was no sign of Empire blood; only a peaceful burnt umber, leaf-green, gold, and the collections of punctuation marks or blots and stains which implied people – living, dying, buried; and then up and down the map all the silver threads that were rivers, real rivers, not English puddles or Spanish valleys where the water had disappeared for so long that people picnicked on the riverbed. Grace could not forget the snow-capped peaks and snowfilled torrents; during her stay in Great Britain she had not been to sit humbly, politely, by a narrow stream beside a hill and afterwards write home about her visit to a river near a mountain. Only Keats could write 'I stood tiptoe upon a little hill', without offending his sensitive countrymen!

The room was cold. Grace lit the gas fire and warmed her hands. She looked out of the window at the darkening Winchley landscape. She touched the clean-shaven dormant potatoes. She pulled her nightdress from her bag and put it under her pillow. Then no longer able to delay the act of sitting to a meal with Philip and Anne, she went slowly downstairs into the kitchen, taking her place as if she had lived with the family all her life; waiting with her mouth slightly open, like a child, like a helpless 'younker', for the dispensed meat pie and peaches.

Philip asked her again if she had a pleasant journey from London. She replied, Yes thank you.

Philip seemed to listen for sounds from upstairs.

—Silence, he said. —This is the best part of the day, when the children are asleep.

—I suppose it is, Grace said.

When people spoke to her she was in the habit of punctuating their remarks with Yes, yes, I see, yes, with sometimes a murmured m-m-m-m. She never said No, no, no. How alarmed she and others would have been had she said No, no, no! no I don't see, I don't understand! But, yes, she saw, she understood, yes yes of course, m-m-m-m.

They ate without speaking, although sometimes Philip turned to glance at Grace as he made a casual guest-warming and including remark. She realised that she had lived almost entirely in a world of blue-eyed people. Philip's eyes were hazel – no, not hazel, nor yellow nor amber; an autumn colouring with flecks like the veins of golden leaves; yet not autumnal – there was something – why, his eyes were like the yellowish flesh of a cooked trout, they had the earthy golden taste too and the soft separation of flesh from bone; there showed in them, too, the innocent meanness of a small boy in a school playground; also a 'brown-eye-pick-the-pie' greed; then a pure truthful wintry concern for clarity, an autumnal dissolving of all foliage, all blossoming masses of obscurity from – say – a grove of thought, landscape of human behaviour.

When Grace studied Philip's eyes she could feel at the back of her mind the movement of sliding doors opening to let out small furry evil-smelling animals with sharp claws and teeth, into the sunlight; Grace could feel the door moving, she sniffed the stench that followed the little animal as it crept inquisitively yet cautiously out of its cage; its bright eyes closed quickly in the glare of the light, then growing used to the new enclosure it opened its eyes and began exploring, until it discovered the wire-netting, the boundaries; it was not free, after all; it had been let out to blink in the sun only while its cage was being cleaned!

———

After dinner Grace went with Philip and Anne to the sitting room where a coal fire was burning. Grace sat in an armchair by the fire near bookshelves filled with books, Philip sat opposite her, while Anne sat facing the fire, a new copy of *Ulysses* open on her lap. Grace studied the books – New Zealand Year Books, New Zealand Histories, New Zealand, New Zealand . . .

She tensed herself for the after-dinner fireside conversation. Philip opened the latest copy of the *Church Times* and began to read.

—Listen to this. You won't like it.

He was talking to Anne who dutifully listened.

—Do you see the *Church Times*, Grace?

—Yes, once or twice.

Philip and Anne did not discuss what Philip had read. Anne returned to her book, Philip to his newspaper, while Grace cast stealthy glances at both, trying to penetrate their secrets.

—Have you read *Ulysses*, Grace?

—Yes, a long time ago.

—However did you manage to read it?

—Oh, Grace said, suddenly terrified that perhaps she had sounded too bold and proud, almost boastful, for evidently one boasted when one had read *Ulysses* —Oh I read it. Of course, she said firmly, lessening her glory, —I didn't understand much of it, but I liked reading it.

—I don't know, Anne said wearily, —how anyone can get through it.

Perceiving in her tone a reference to housewifery, motherhood, life in Winchley, as well as to the reading of *Ulysses*, Philip looked warmly at her, and with an in-spite-of-Winchley-and-all cheering note in his voice he said to Grace,

—Anne's been very good, you know; she attends a WEA course on Modern Novels, and they're studying James Joyce. She's been doing a hell of a lot of reading. She's been awfully good.

He looked admiringly at Anne. He had spoken rather loudly, as if to drown the voice of Winchley-and-all.

Meanwhile Grace was dividing her mind between studying Philip and Anne and their life together, and trying to arrange, ready for its appearance in speech, the truth of her relationship with *Ulysses*. She found that her memory had placed *Ulysses*, not under the heading of Literature, but in the file which held the embarrassing and painful facts of College Life.

She read *Ulysses* at College. Roll-call – Childs, Cleave, Coster, Crawley – the only names, apart from the usual brilliant, beautiful or eccentric characters, that she could remember from the alphabetical roll-call. She had not even a clear image of the Childs, Coster, Crawley which surrounded her – Childs played hockey, was a 'sporting type'; Coster was a swot, clever at making puppets; Crawley . . . Grace could remember nothing of her personally, only that she came from Timaru, the rival of Grace's hometown – Oamaru, and she remained in Grace's mind more a symbol of Timaru than a human being, so much that if Grace thought of Crawley (Joyce? Noeline? Bertha?) she thought at once of Caroline Bay, its rivalry with Oamaru's Friendly Bay, and the humiliation suffered by Oamaru when each year in the Tourist Guides Caroline Bay was praised, Friendly Bay ignored. Why, Grace used to think, sitting moodily in a geomorphology lecture, Friendly Bay has everything, Caroline Bay has nothing, nothing, nothing. Yet through her two years at College, and long afterwards, Childs, Coster, and the Crawley from Timaru, acted as escorts to Grace's name.

But *Ulysses*. Oh. Grace remembered *Ulysses*, but again it was not the book which claimed her memory. It was the realisation that the strangeness and insecurity of the late war years, spent at school and college, were epitomised most vividly and terribly, for Grace, in the paper on which books of those years were printed: pale yellow speckled paper where the printed word seemed just another blemish that could be attributed, in the preface, to War-Time Economy. Grace remembered that opening such books filled her with terror and foreboding; it seemed as if an end had come to everything, that nothing mattered any more; books had seemed, in some way, the last hope, and now that language had become as an excusable stain upon a piece of coarse kitchen towelling, there was no hope left.

At that moment Grace thought, What if Philip's eyes with their dark flecks are reminding me of the print upon yellow sheets of war-time economy paper?

—Oh, she said suddenly and foolishly, —Oh it's quiet here, there's no traffic!

Philip and Anne stopped their reading to look tolerantly at her.

—Yes, you'll find it a change, Anne said, returning to *Ulysses*.

—Winchley's quiet, Philip agreed, opening *The Spectator*.

—I notice, he said, that the critics are ceasing to be indulgent towards every Russian writer who is published here. Some are even turning against *Doctor Zhivago*. I didn't care terribly for it myself.

—Oh I liked it, Anne said. —It made me weep. Of course, I was pregnant at the time.

—If you read it when you were pregnant and wept over it then perhaps the critics – Grace began.

Philip finished her sentence, laughing.

—Perhaps the critics were pregnant?

—Did you read it, Grace?

—Yes, no, I mean yes. I don't read many novels.

—Professional jealousy?

—Perhaps; yes.

—I hope your coming for the weekend is not interrupting anything you're working on.

—Oh no, Oh no.

Grace continued her study of the books near her, choosing one from time to time, reading a little, then replacing it. She felt tired. She wanted to go home to London, to the flat, to sit at her typewriter; she wanted to sleep; to turn her face away from the street-lights and close her eyes.

—Philip has plenty of New Zealand books.

—Yes.

She opened the *Book of New Zealand Verse* which in New Zealand she had always kept by her bed but which she had been unable to read during her stay in Great Britain. She touched the familiar red cover, noting with pleasure the clear bold printing, the beautiful m's and n's like archways, the lintel t's, the delicately-throated r's . . . She glanced through the long introductory essay, a self-conscious loving dedication to 'these islands', and then began to read some of the poems.

'I am the nor'west air nosing among the pines'
I am . . .
'I am . . . the rust on railway lines . . .
cows called to milking . . . the magpie's screech'

———

So I, a migratory bird, am suffering from the need to return to the place I have come from before the season and sun are right for my return. Do I meet spring summer or winter? Here I live in a perpetual other season unable to read in the sky, the sun, the temperature, the signs for returning. Is it homesickness – 'I know a place whereon . . .' the matagouri, the manuka, the cabbage tree grow . . .

I know a place.

Grace said to herself, I found my first place when I was three. It is a memory that is so deep in my mind that it is always and never changing. I went by myself into the dusty road. It was late summer, the gorse flowers in the hedge were turning brown at the tips of their petals, crumpling and dropping. The sky was grey with a few white clouds hurried along by the wind. There were no people anywhere, not up or down the dusty road. I looked up and down and along and over and there was no one. This is *my* place, I thought, standing still, listening. The wind moaned in the telegraph wires and the white dust whirled along the road and I stood in *my* place feeling more and more lonely because the gorse hedge and its flowers were mine, the dusty road was mine, and the wind and the moaning it made through the telegraph wires. I cannot describe the sense of loneliness I felt when I knew that I was in my place; it was early to learn the burden of possession, to own something that couldn't be given away or disowned, that had to be kept for ever. I remember that I didn't stay long in *my* place: I cried and I ran home, but my place followed me like a shadow and it is always near me, even here in Winchley, and I do not even need to close my eyes or call for silence before I am there, and once there wanting to escape from the message of the wind for there is no one up or down along and over and it is dust, not people, that whirls its busy life along the road.

I remember that a year later I found another place which was mine. I found it, that is, I set out to look for it; it was given to me; I took possession of it. We had moved to a new district in the south (as ever) – a wilderness of sheep, cattle, the dark damp growth and precipitating water of gullies; swamps, tussock; few people. The railway house was there on the hill waiting for us to move in. We children had stomped about in every room making the wooden floors echo with our heavy rhythm of occupation. Men were carrying the furniture up the hill; my mother was 'seeing to' cups of tea for everybody; there were bursts of excitement, temper, tears, as we planned the first night when we always slept, in a new house, in a mattress bed on the floor with the blackpainted and scraped iron bedends with their screw-on brass knobs (in which we placed our communications in code) and the rusty wire mattress leaning against the wall, ready to be hammered together the next day. —Mum, have you got the bed-key? Where's the bed-key? Why can't we always sleep on the floor?

I'll tan your bottoms the lot of you . . .

56

Suddenly finding myself alone and dissatisfied with the possession of a new house, I went down the front steps through the grass-overgrown garden into a paddock (sheep looked at me, their heads on one side, their long noble faces thoughtful, their eyes narrow, slit with bits of licorice; their bodies were bunched and overclothed like Mrs Daniel, one of our neighbours in the last town we'd lived in). I walked a short way into another paddock, along a gully until I came to a clump of silver-birch trees, some dead, or dying, with new leaves sprouting from their sprawled trunks. I walked into the green and silver darkness their leaves made. I scuffed the deep pile of old leaves, my shoes sinking through the fresh layer of whole leaves, through last year's, through those of the year before and the year before until I uncovered the decayed leaves of any year or no year; they were no longer leaves; they were earth. I sat on one of the tree-trunks. I smelled the leaves and the silver and green enclosed air, and I knew, with a surge of pleasure inside me, that I had set out to look for *my* place, and that I had found it, that I had chosen it. There was no need for me to put up a sign that it was my place. My place. I had chosen it.

I returned happily to the new house (what did it matter who slept next to the wall, for safety, and who slept next to the door, to be grabbed in the night by bogies?). I told no one of my new possession. I did not visit the place ever again, for the new chosen possession brought its own burden – had I chosen something which would stay, or would it disappear; could I take it with me and shed it when I wished; what was it that I had chosen? I still remember the pleasure of finding it and owning it; it seemed then like a little birch-tree house; it seems now like layers of years that sink deep, like leaves, into rich fertile decay.

And now what confusion I feel when I sit here and read these poems. All the poets are writing about *my* place. Even if

they were not writing of New Zealand they would be writing
of my place. How can I ever contain within me so much of
one land? Was it given to me or have I looked for it, found it,
and have I been afraid to return to it?

> '. . . and from their haunted bay
> The godwits vanish towards another summer . . .
> distance looks our way . . .'

—Reading New Zealand poetry?
—Yes.
—I suppose you've met some of the poets?
—Yes, I've met some.
Silence.
—I think, Grace said, —I'll retire now – go to bed.
—Will you have coffee first?
They drank coffee, made and brought in by Anne. Grace
returned to the shelves the books which she had accumulated
around her, choosing, opening, shutting. She glanced again at
the *Book of New Zealand Verse*.

> 'A *View of Rangitoto*
>
> . . . But the mountain still lives out that fiercer life
> Beneath its husk of darkness; blind to the age
> Scuttling by it over shiftless waters,
>
> The cold beams that wake upon its headlands
> To usher night-dazed ships. For it belongs to
> A world of fire before the rocks and waters.'

Grace made a wild movement with her hand as if she were
trying to lift the volcano from between the pages, to carry it

upstairs to her room. I know Rangitoto, she said to herself. I know Rangitoto.

But of course she did not know it. People in Auckland turned to gaze at it, to point and say, The shape is peculiar; from whichever angle it is viewed it appears the same; it is Auckland's landmark, her phenomenon.

They gazed and gazed at it, but they did not know it, and Grace did not know it, yet she had learned to set poetic bearings by it; its outer sameness concealed its inner surprise.

Ah, she thought, I knew someone, once, a great favourite with all. I asked Why. I was told, He's always the same, isn't he, always the same!

No it wasn't God.

———

—Goodnight.

—See you in the morning, Philip said, almost as if he did not expect to see her.

—Yes, Grace said.

When she had reached the top of the stairs, and had opened the door to her room and walked in, she could no longer pretend; she shrugged away the commonplace Yes No I see I understand, she cried No, No, No, I'm a migratory bird.

'. . . and from their haunted bay
The godwits vanish towards another summer.
Everywhere in light and calm the murmuring
Shadow of departure; distance looks our way;
And none knows where he will lie down at night.'

PART TWO

Another Summer

8

I remember, she said to herself, lying in the cold dark room at Winchley.

—Before I was born the Leith river flooded and the house in Leith Street where my mother and father, his parents, my sister and brother lived, was flooded too, and although the house was not abandoned the flood was serious enough to become one of the vivid memories of our lives – even of *my* life; it was talked of, dreamed of, it had been captured in photographs that were studied long after we had moved from Dunedin to Outram; when I was small I shared it with the family as our most recent disastrous memory.

—There's Grandad standing at the door of the house in Leith Street. That was taken just after the flood.

—There's Leith Street. During the flood. People sailed up and down the street in tables.

—There's Dad and Isy and Jim. Before the flood.

—There's Grandma. See, in her wheelchair she's safe from the flood.

Grandma had diabetes, and one of her legs had been cut off. Sometimes she wore a wooden leg but she could move faster in her wheelchair.

I had learned so much about the flood, it had become so much a part of my memory that I was dismayed to learn that I hadn't experienced it, and my dismay increased when I realised that Isy and Jim, my big sister and brother, could use the flood as a weapon against me. Ya, Ya, you weren't in the flood!

—But I remember it, I said.

—You weren't born. We've got photos of us in the flood, but you weren't born.

I knew that not being born at the right time I had missed something important, especially as I confused the Leith flood with the other flood so often talked of by my mother, where it rained forty days and nights, an ark was built, and the animals were rescued two by two. How I envied Isy and Jim their meeting with all the animals in the world, for I knew only the cattle and sheep in the paddocks, and in the cowbyre where I sat in my gocart I knew Betty the bigboned red and white cow with the long horns. I watched while my mother milked her. When I was old enough and had graduated from the gocart, had served my term in the petrol-box under the walnut tree (each new baby had a petrol-box to crawl, play, and learn to walk in), I used to stand in front of the bail throwing potatoes to Betty, and I used to gather the apples from under the trees in the orchard to feed to her. My grandma sang,

'The animals went in two by two,
One more river to cross.
One more river, and that's the river to Jordan . . .'

and I wished that she would not sing it, for I hadn't been there, and I couldn't remember the animals, and the idea of going to Jordan frightened me, and my mother talked of the *Red Sea* and the *Dead Sea*, and the only river I knew was the *Taieri*. Why hadn't I been born earlier, so that I *knew*?

I grew up. I passed into the grownup territory of playing, which Isy and Jim had already made their own – the engine sheds, the goods sheds by the 'railway', and farther along the road the drill-hall at the back of which was stored a 'magazine', always spoken of with dread. We were forbidden to go near the magazine. We did not know the nature of it but the word filled us with terror. Magazine. Whenever we went out to play my mother warned us, 'Remember there's a *magazine* at the back of the drill-hall!'

We played in the 'good-shed', chasing each other up and down the sacks of wheat which we called 'climbers'. It was about then that I became, by dictionary definition, 'a thievish small bird haunting church towers' – a jackdaw. My wings were black, my beak was yellow, my cry was a screech which frightened Isy and Jim as nothing had frightened them before, or perhaps they pretended to be afraid; nevertheless I was happy and powerful, I could live at the top of the climbers, near the roof, and suddenly appearing from behind a big climber, I would flap my wings, thrust forward my yellow beak and fly out to seize Isy and Jim,

—I'm a jackdaw, I'm a jackdaw!

And how proud I felt when we were called for dinner and we trooped in and sat at the table and Isy and Jim, in answer to

—What've you been doing this morning?

gave the most important item of our play,

—Grace is a jackdaw.

Yes, Grace is a jackdaw.

I don't know for how long I remained a jackdaw; perhaps long enough to gain my self-respect which was shattered every time the famous flood was mentioned.

———

How does an only child manage without the social education of brothers and sisters? I lived in what the *Free Lance* or the *Weekly News* would describe as a 'social whirl': sister, brother, aunts, uncles, grandmother, grandfather, ordinary neighbours

65

like Mr and Mrs Widdowson, Mr and Mrs Brown; people who worked with my father or provided our groceries or lent us their bull or talked over the fence to my mother, or whose children entered our lives with their invitations, 'Come on over to our place' – 'our place' being miles away; and beyond the ordinary neighbours the powerful important people who gave orders which could frighten, heal, imprison, dismiss (the 'sack'): policemen, doctors, mayors, councillors; then, beyond these 'important people' the remote persons whose names were printed in the 'paper' – the King, the Prince of Wales, Gandhi, Mr Forbes, Mr Coates; murderers, actors, thieves, artists, foreign emperors; and beyond all, God. When the thought of God came to your mind it was so swift that there was no time to examine it. —Who made the World? your playmate said, and you answered, —God.

His quelling power in response to arguments was tremendous; you won if you could say 'God said' or 'God did'; it was even more useful than the 'Dad said', 'Dad did' so often used to gain the advantage.

If beyond the family there was a 'social whirl', nearer home, life was so heavily populated that it almost became a social dizziness: besides relatives – grandparents who lived with us, aunts, uncles, cousins who came for holidays, a mother, a father, two sisters now, one brother – there were spiders in the corners of the floor and roof, slaters and slugs under stones, worms in the garden, ladybirds on leaves, snails in the bushes, birds in the trees, rats and mice in the scullery, trout in the river, cattle and sheep in the paddocks, and our new cow Beauty, smaller, less wild and tossing than Betty who, my mother explained, was 'an Ayreshire, not as trustworthy and gentle as a Jersey'. It was my job now to feed Beauty with potatoes while she was being milked. She stood pinned in the bail slowly chewing her cud or slicing and crunching the black-eyed potatoes. Sometimes when a potato dropped from the heap away from her she would stretch her neck forward, open her mouth, blowing out her grassy breath, and roll out her long signal-red tongue like a passage carpet even to the curled tip that will not uncurl and lie flat. Then having regained the straying potato Beauty would begin munching it, drawing her head back towards the bail, with the golden and black skin of her neck which had so obligingly allowed her to stretch for the lost potato, settling to its habitual saggy folds; then Beauty would close her eyes dreaming, swish her tail, while spitter-spatter went the milk into the bucket until the bucket was full, and the white foam overflowed.

—

When I stopped being a jackdaw I withdrew for a time from the 'social whirl' and became a solitary 'beastie' in the paddock. I even wore a 'beastie' dress of gold velvet, and although I had often been afraid of the beasties in their coats of gold velvet I was no longer afraid when I had my own beastie dress. All day I explored and played in the paddock; alone with the beasties, until something happened to frighten my mother and father who looked at each other and said, talking of me, —She's been playing near the swamp. Oh, the swamp! Red weed grew on it, the same colour as the inside of the red rubber ball which an aunt had given to us 'brand-new' and which we had torn to pieces because our curiosity about its inside had grown so intense we could bear it no longer, we *had* to know what it was made of and where its bounce came from. Our aunt had been so angry when she returned for a visit and saw the bounceless red rubber wreck lying neglected on the garden path.

But if we hadn't destroyed the red rubber ball how should we have known that the swamp in the next paddock had weed identical with the inside of the ball?

67

It seemed that, like the 'magazine', the swamp was a forbidden place. There were so many places and things
forbidden and to be feared – the flood, the war, the magazine,
the swamp, bulls, rats in the wall, drunk men, swaggers, the
strap, uncles and aunts who threatened, 'We'll put you in a
sack and throw you in the sea.' 'The gypsies will steal you.'
Also, there were our own little knotted handkerchiefs which
held our treasured collection of childhood beliefs and super-
stitions – mixtures of truth and fantasy, of words misheard or
misunderstood, of half-solved perplexities, of desperate questions given desperate answers rather than be left with no
answer at all . . . my eye was hurt . . . the doctor made it
better, the doctor and the pixies whom I called the 'pitties'.
Who were the 'pitties'? Why did my mother smile when I
talked of them? Why did she keep asking me, as if she didn't
know, —Who made your eye better? and when I answered,
preferring the stranger explanation, —The 'pitties', why did
she look so pleased and sly?

I could not speak properly; words were confused. One of my
favourite toys was a kerosene tin with a piece of rope tied to it,
which I pulled along the lawn under the walnut tree and over
to the fence for the beasties to share my pleasure in it. There
was a song which I sang about my tin, but why did everyone
laugh when I sang it?

> 'God save our gracious tin,
> God save our noble tin,
> God save the tin.'

Words were so mysterious, full of pleasure and fear. Mosgiel.
Mosgiel. Up Central. Taieri. Waihola. Ao-Tea-Roa. Lottie.
Lottie. That was my mother's name, yet we never called her
Lottie, it was only aunts and uncles who were allowed to use
her name.

My aunt, who had her goitre out (goitre, goitre), stood at the door, in the passage, and called,

—Oh Lottie, one moment, Lottie.

Or she said to my father,

—What does Lottie think? Does Lottie like living in Outram?

Sometimes when visitors came the word would come strangely from my father's lips and with a feeling of shock I would try to believe that he had said it.

—As I was saying to Lottie only this afternoon . . .

The word was strange and frightening; it gave my mother a new distinction which seemed to separate her from us, which implied that she did not belong to us at all. It made me curious about her and jealous of her; her name was a way of saying *No to us* – but weren't we her babies, hadn't I been her special baby until Dorry was born? And when the next one was born wouldn't it be her special baby too? A terrible panic overwhelmed me when I heard her name; I saw her moving farther and farther away; I knew it was true, she didn't belong to us at all and we didn't belong to her, and I was myself, only myself and nobody else.

Sometimes I repeated her name softly. Lottie. Once I called her name aloud and she became angry and my father said,

—Don't be rude to your mother. Lottie and George. Lottie-and-George. They were my mother and father. No one but us called them Mum and Dad.

I played by myself, near the fence, while the beastie stood looking at me. As beasties do, it was weeping, a tear running down the thin dark track upon its cheek. I spoke to it.

—Lottie, I said. —How you do you like living in Outram?

Then very boldly I called out, —Lottie-and-George, Lottie-and-George!

———

—I've had a shift, my father said. —We're going to live in Glenham. People 'on the railway' were always 'shifting', and when my mother talked to the neighbours somewhere in the conversation there would be reference to 'being on the railway' and 'shifting'. Yet I think my mother was pleased when we were settled in Glenham for it was not as close as Outram had been to the Main Trunk Line, and my father did not have the responsibility of being on the expresses. He had not long been promoted from Fireman to Engine-driver and here, out in the country, there was little danger of his driving head-on into another train or running over some of the thousands and thousands of people who lived near Dunedin. My mother calmed her fears and sang to us at night when my father had gone to work (carrying his handmade leather work-bag, his engine-driver cap, his blueys, his salmon sandwiches)

'Daddy's on the engine,
don't be afraid.'

So it was all right. We were not afraid. And if my father were driving the engine near our house he always blew the whistle to let us know that all was well.

I slept in the cot now; it was still my size. Dorry, the baby, was getting bigger and would soon be ready to leave her petrol-box and join my sister and brother and me in our new world of Glenham and the Glenham railway, among the old twisted rusty lines, the piled sleepers, the disused turntable . . .

Soon it would be time for the stork to bring another baby, but it was not quite time, for Dorry still fed at my mother's titties and slept between my mother and father in the 'big bed'. Perhaps on our next shift, my mother said, there might be a new baby, but I was not interested, for Dorry belonged to me, my mother had told me so, and it wasn't likely that I could have two, so soon; there were my sister and brother to think of, and dividing had to be strictly fair.

Sooner than my father expected he was given another transfer – to Edendale, not far from Glenham. The surprising and exciting novelty about this 'shift' was that our house was to accompany us; it was to be dismantled, carried to Edendale, and rebuilt, and while we were waiting we were to live in railway huts in Glenham.

It was winter, and it snowed, and because Glenham was inland the snow stayed and became deeper and deeper. Our huts were set in the snow. One hut belonged to my mother and father and the baby, one hut was our bedroom, another a kitchen, sitting room, another a washhouse.

My father dug a dumpy about fifty yards from the huts and built a tin shed to cover it. We lived here for six months. We had colds that did not get better, we were 'steamed' with Friar's Balsam, my legs ached and I cried and cried, and the aunt from Dunedin visited and said Lottie how can you put up with it, and the world was full of beetles, beetles crawling up the wall and along the ceiling and the floor and I said Look at the beetles and my mother said Where, and I pointed to them, and the aunt from Dunedin said,

—She's delirious.

It snowed and snowed. There were rats whispering in the wall; there were strange shadows creeping up and down the wall; if we were afraid in the night or had toothache we could not get to our mother and father, for it was dark outside and the snow was too deep. The baby had a funny little cough like a sheep's cough and her face was red and shiny; my mother's arms and hands were red with washing clothes and nappies. Sometimes my mother would talk wistfully to my father or to us of the time in Outram when she had her 'arm up' for six weeks and 'your father did the washing and milked the cow'.

I couldn't remember about my mother's hurting her arm and having it bandaged, but I sensed that it was an important occasion in her life, almost as important as the flood, and rivalled only by the now legendary time that my father had his 'ankle in plaster' following an accident at football in Dunedin.

—When I was off with my ankle, my father used to say.

I was always disappointed to learn that my father's ankle had been hurt at football; it seemed unworthy. And I was always sad when my mother talked of her arm, she talked so wistfully, as if it had been a time of great freedom that she would never again experience – yet how was it freedom if her arm had been in a sling?

—When you were little, and I had my arm up for six weeks . . .

———

Our house was built and we had scarcely time to get used to it when another 'shift' came: to Wyndham, the largest town we had lived in – with one Main Street and a few other streets, with 'over the fence' neighbours; a school, a river; and people, people everywhere. It was an exciting day when we moved (not forgetting to take Beauty with us) into the house beside the railway line in Ferry Street. There were houses all the way along the road to the river at one end and the main street at the other. From a world of snowgrass, snowberries, manuka, cattle, sheep, birds, with only sky and rabbits and paddocks for miles and miles, to streets with houses and people; people to know, to stare at, to poke faces at, to call names after, to be afraid of, to run from.

I was four. We explored under the house and found it 'good'. An open cow-bail was made for Beauty in the corner of the garden near the railway line. Down the end of the garden there was a pump for our water. Over the fence near the pump was another railway house where the Hadfords lived – Mr, Mrs, Mavis, Joan, Ronnie. Now that we were surrounded by people my mother seemed to lose her wistfulness; she became a busy neighbour accepting and giving hot scones, pikelets, jams; exchanging views; and, inside our home, expressing her opinion of the neighbours – the Hadfords, the Lyles, the Bakers. Although she talked to our father and not to us, we listened and learned. To our pride we learned that we had 'strong little chests' whereas Mavis Hadford was definitely consumptive and Ronnie was like a stick and the Baker children were like sticks and what they all needed was plenty of milk and cream. Their frailty, my mother said, came from their living 'in the town'. If living in Wyndham was living in 'the town' then we children liked it, and however longingly and proudly my mother soon began to talk of 'when we lived in the huts, six months in winter, in snow, when Dorry was a baby' we wouldn't have exchanged Wyndham for Glenham or Edendale or Outram. We played with the Hadfords and the Bakers. We played neighbours and visiting and school and I was the teacher and my mother looked from the kitchen door and I heard her saying to Mrs Lyles who had come to borrow some flour, —She'll be a schoolteacher when she grows up!

Life in Wyndham was full of excitement! Ronnie Hadford pushed a bead up his nose and couldn't get it down again; Mavis Hadford broke her leg and was sent to hospital and when she came home she had crutches and we said —Lend us your crutches Mavis, and she was so mean about lending them, and we tried to use one of Grandma's crutches for playing broken legs but hers were not the right size, therefore we made ourselves stilts instead, walking up and down Ferry Street on stilts until Isy slipped and a protruding nail tore her shin.

—My shin, she said.

Shin. Shin. The doctor sewed it, leaving a white scar, and

for a time my mother talked of another accident which happened to Isy before I was born.

—When Isy was a baby and drank Jeyes Fluid and I gave her an emetic.

An emetic?

—I gave her an emetic and rushed her to the doctor.

Oh my mother was so brave and so swift! Tommy Lyles was a ganger on the railway, and the train ran over him outside our house and my mother tore up sheets to bandage him, almost as if she had been waiting all her life for an opportunity to tear up sheets. It was always happening; the newspaper was always telling of people who ran to the scene of the accident and tore up sheets. After this accident my mother was not inclined to talk about it. She did not make it another occasion of her life – 'When Tommy Lyles was run over and I tore up sheets and you were little', because Tommy Lyles died.

We avoided playing near the railway line where Tommy Lyles was killed, and we looked with awe at the house where he had lived, and we stared at Mrs Lyles because she had been his wife, and once in the night I pulled aside the curtain and looked out of the window at their house to surprise it in the darkness, to see if it had changed and showed the change only at night, but I could see nothing significant about it, it was an ordinary railway house, like ours except that a cabbage tree grew on the front lawn.

For weeks after Tommy Lyles' death the rumour of death stayed in the air. My mother would suddenly put her hand over her heart, gasp, and look afraid. People seemed to want to say, Look what happened to Tommy Lyles. And we who used to like to go on the side of the railway line to pick the wild sweet peas, stopped going there because Tommy Lyles had been there. Of course we had never called him Tommy. He was Mr Lyles. Sometimes in my mind I heard my father say

74

with a terrible doom in his voice, —Mum, Tommy Lyles died on the way to hospital.

—Don't, Curly.

You see it was my father who drove the train that killed him.

It was War now, and wounds, not football wounds. Having so many neighbours we now had more visitors, a Mr and Mrs from here and there almost every night, and while my mother talked about children and the government with the women, the men exchanged reminiscences of the War. My father adopted a special voice for speaking of the War.

—Yes, we were in the War. We were in the trenches.

—Oh, the trenches. Don't Curly, my mother would say, growing pale and putting her hand over her heart. I wasn't sure what the trenches were but I knew they must be terrible places.

—Mademoiselle from Armentierres, *parley-vu*, my father sang. Pack Up your Troubles in your old Kit Bag and smile, smile, smile. Carry me back to Blighty.

I found it very strange and frightening to be at the War with my father singing

'I want to go home
I want to go home,
I don't want to go to the trenches no more
where the bullets and shrapnel are flying galore.
Take me over the sea
where the Allemand won't get at me,
Oh my,
I don't want to die,
I want to go home!'

We all knew that when our father sang that song he was at the War; there was something in the song which mattered here, now, in Ferry Street Wyndham Southland South Island New Zealand Southern Hemisphere the World the Universe; the meaning of what mattered showed in the two lines,

'Oh my, I don't want to die,
I want to go home!'

When I heard the song I knew by the way my father sang and the expression on his face that he was afraid to die, and when my mother heard him singing I knew by her face that she didn't ever want my father to die but she was afraid that per-haps – who knows – look what happened to Tommy Lyles – perhaps he might die, any day, today, tomorrow . . .

—Don't Curly, she said, —Don't sing that. You're not at the War now.

Mostly they talked of the War as if it were a place set far across the sea, like San Francisco or Honolulu, and every few years in history soldiers travelled there to be there and when you talked of all the soldiers who had ever fought in all the years you spoke of them as having been 'at the Wars'. Many of the fairy-tales began, 'An old soldier, home from the Wars'. They went away as young boys, they came home aged, with grey hair, wooden legs and walking sticks . . .

Yet from the way people talked I knew the War wasn't a place like San Francisco or Honolulu, it was something which moved like an iceberg or a cloud; it was invisible, not moving in the same direction, like a river or keeping the same shape like a train on the railway line, but always changing, perhaps growing arms and legs and a face then losing them or having them blotted out; perhaps putting down a root into the garden or the road or into water – the sea, rivers, and staying there, growing tall, blossoming, then withering; blown here and there by the wind; entering people, becoming people, stealing from them, adding to them, changing the shape of their lives:

that was the War. It pursued forever, while people tried to escape from it; they sang Pack Up your Troubles and Oh My I don't want to die, I want to go home.

But was there anywhere to go? How could you go home if you were already home?

Or was home some place out of the world?

Sometimes I thought it would be comforting and convenient to find such a place.

Especially when

      a. you had toothache.

      b. you would soon be starting school.

9

Grace got out of bed and switched off the gas fire. The flames ceased their whispering, the rosy-icing latticework paled, the room was cold as if there had been no fire. The waiting frost fingered the windowpane, slid open trapdoors of glass, crept into the room touching the four corners with a permanent night chill, stroking Grace's pillow which then stayed cold all night. She switched on the bedlamp and climbed again into the cold bed. Her bones were aching with cold; she drew her breath, gasping, through her teeth. Then unable to bear the discomfort she went to the wardrobe drawer, found an extra blanket and returned to bed, wrapping the blanket around her between the sheets. Ah; her skin began to glow with warmth. Anne and Philip will be warm, she thought. The word obsessed her. Warm. Warmth. She tried to remember a time when the sun had not been absent; it seemed impossible to think of any colours other than grey, white, black. And the children will be warm, she thought, for children have special supplies. I have no rubber bottle, electric blanket; only a cardigan and a woollen blanket between the sheets; human skin is best and simplest.

Yet Grace was enjoying the cold, now that it was barred from entering her bed. Currents of clear cold thought flowed through her head. She remembered that the room and bed belonged to Anne's father. How often he must lie here, she thought, feeling the cold and not being willing to admit it, gazing at the ceiling and the walls, the New Zealand pictures, Wakatipu, the Southern Alps, Christchurch; tasting the warm wind blowing across the plains; lying here, rigid and stern knowing that a lifetime of memories of one land has shrunk from the vast spaces of mountains, plains and bush-valleys to this white-painted austere room. Surely the few possessions which he chose to bring from New Zealand must be so burdened with their concentration of memories that at times he cannot bear to inspect them in this remote northern Winchley light, without suffering a corresponding heaviness of heart. Yet how noble he must feel, having made his choice, having reduced the clutter of his life to one room.

Grace noted the framed photograph of Anne; rosy, dark-haired, smiling; perhaps a graduation photograph bearing the innocence, the blurred milky naiveté which seem typical of photos taken in your youth, in your home town, and which are never again captured, especially if you leave your home town to spend your life in another country. Grace supposed that Anne might not care for this photo; there was an unsophisticated eagerness about it which was not so much the direct responsibility of the photographer as of the home town atmosphere, which, naturally charged with family history and secrets, and with provincial prides and concerns, had seeped into the photograph in the same way that it spilled in the streets and the houses and their furniture and revealed itself absorbed in the faces of the people.

Grace remembered a first book by an Australian writer, how the photo on the jacket had been eager, innocent as the photo of Anne; again, it was not only the woman herself, it was her home town, her family, her life. When the writer left Australia to live in England and there published another book with her photo on the jacket, how changed she appeared in the photograph, how discreet the camera had been, telling its truth through its small selective lies; freed from the narrow repressive restrictions of home town atmosphere. The writer appeared tidier, more fashionable, sophisticated; you would almost not have known her from other writers, you could have placed her photo beside others of the same type and tidiness and not have been able to distinguish one from the other – like those cemeteries which are planned as Gardens of Rest and when you walk among the roses and dahlias and gladioli, knowing that so many ashes are buried in the garden, you can't really allot the dead their correct place – the blades of grass on the lawn seem so much alike, and you can't pluck the petals from the roses to find which has been nourished by Mary, Henry, George, Wilfred.

If photos of the writer, of Anne, and of Grace herself were taken now, Grace thought, all would show this discretion of which Death is master; one might grieve for the old home town photos, but the new had their advantages . . .

Grace had been reaching to switch off the bedlamp when Anne's photo had distracted her; now she settled back into the darkness, snuggled into the woollen blanket, pulled the bedclothes almost over her head and closed her eyes. No sound from the children's room. Philip and Anne had not yet gone to bed.

What were they talking about, down there by the fire?

Grace tried not to think of her failure to communicate by speech; she traced her part in the evening's conversation. If only she had said this, if only she had said that! Why did she always seem to stop in midsentence and not know how to continue because her words and ideas had vanished?

She began to cry, quietly, and cried herself to sleep.

10

Once or twice she woke, drew the bedclothes down to free her arms and turned from the wall to the dark glistening shape of window. Immediately the chilling air surged near her, touching spears of icicles upon her skin; she lay entombed in ice; anyone coming into the room would have seen the oblong coffin-shape of ice resting upon the bed containing deep within it the smoky darkening-blue feminine shape of a comfortless week-ender, migratory bird, lying in the penultimate home of an elderly New Zealand sheep-farmer. Country darkness fills the bowl of light to overflowing; in city darkness little silver lights swim like fish in and around the pool. Winchley at night was dark and lonely. No sound. No moreporks, hedgehogs, cats, no sea crashing over the breakwater, town-clock striking the quarter-hour. No people; only now and again from the children's room the small restless whimpers which children make in their dreams – Don't take it from me, it's mine, Mummy, Noel's got it, and it's mine, I want this, I want this, but it belongs to Sarah, No No I want it, Mummy look what Noel's doing, Daddy what's Grace-Cleave staying here for, where's my baby Jesus and my angels: whimpers for things broken or stolen or put out of reach; things things.

No sound from Philip and Anne; they must be deep asleep. They must have accepted their sleeping, performing the ritual of it with the deceiving simplicity of mime, like film stars on the screen – each entering the room, undressing, each drawing back the blankets, lying neatly on the appointed side of the double bed, resting the head just so on the pillow, apart, as if poisonous thorns lay between them; then reaching to switch off the lamp, calling a sporty Cheerio, Night-Night; the eyes closed; the two unmixed in instant sleep. Grace used to imagine, when she saw such modest films, that as soon as the camera had left the scene the bedmates flicked open their eyes, like dolls, and seeing in the dark, sprang towards each other, arms and legs locked like complicated mechanical toys, blood-red and snow-white twisted and exposed, revolving like the colours on a barber's pole. Grace knew that more often it was the unreal film which was real, that a man and woman climbed into bed, arranged the bedclothes considerately with each having a fair share, put out the light, said Ta-Ta or Bye-Bye or See You Tomorrow, and slept, stretched like corpses, as if each were thinking of death and of the trouble and expense that would be saved if they died in the night with their bodies discreetly and properly arranged each to fit its own coffin.

Now and then Grace heard a sigh or murmur from Philip or Anne; something spoken in a dream. I am the perpetual eavesdropper, Grace thought; always with my ear to the wall of other people's lives; such a vicarious existence does not seem possible. I feel that if I were human and not, now, thankfully, a migratory bird, I should be one of the first programmed human machines, with my cold eyes flashing their lights at stated intervals, and my mouth emitting its cardboard code.

Reluctantly she got out of bed and used the chamber, a big roomy vessel with deep white walls like the cliffs of Dover. The British, she thought, are so hospitable.

———

A child crying. —Mummy, Mummy. Sound of sleepy voices from the parents' room, the slow dream-movement of Anne along the passage, Philip stating formally as if thus he could win the inevitable argument with waking, —It's five o'clock in the morning.

Silence once more. Sarah had gone into the big bed between Mummy and Daddy where all three, neither film stars nor corpses, asked for and received the second helping of instant sleep that is a treasured mixture to tired fathers and mothers and children. From a gift of empathy accumulated as the prize and compensation for loneliness, for being denied human essence, forced to live as a migratory bird, Grace was able to help herself to the family mixture of peace after weariness, and she slept, waking into daylight to the hearty recitative of the Village Blacksmith, that is, of Noel, who was using his own language and combination of tunes to sing – one supposed – the praises of waking, thinking of food, light, play, battle, love.

But . . . *sugar-puffs*. Are not these the common denominator of waking?

11

Saturday breakfast. Mistaking the time, too early as usual, Grace came downstairs and found Anne feeding the children their sugar-puffs. Strangely unable to apologise for her intrusion, feeling powerless and spellbound and childlike, she too sat at the table, waiting, her mouth open, like a small bird, for her share of sugar-puffs; and naturally, as if Grace were indeed a child, Anne set about preparing the place in front of her, allotting Grace her spoon, knife, plate, cup and saucer, while Grace looked around her at the morning view that is always so different, so inescapable, shadowless compared with the sleepy stored memory of the night of arrival.

Grace gave a shudder. The day ahead seemed so long, so everlastingly, intolerably provided with light; there was nowhere to hide; even the grey northern light penetrating the kitchen was unmerciful in the way it marked the outline of every object bringing to the furniture and clothes a winter share of poverty and to the face of Anne and the children an incongruous mark of age and defeat. The walls and windows and roofs of houses in the north, Grace observed, were no defence against intruders; the severe winter was overpowering furniture and people as well as trees and hedges and grass. She understood suddenly what might have been the reason for her parents' alarm when as children they used to play in the paddocks and when they came home their mother or father would greet them almost with fear.

—I hope you're not bringing in anything from outside!

She understood, suddenly, the terror of 'outside', the battles waged against it, the comfort and deep bliss felt by those who slept the first night in the first cave; yet even then they had to contend with creatures and 'things' from outside; no wonder a man might become insane with the fear that his last harbour, his private thoughts and dreams, could offer him no shelter.

—Sarah, run upstairs and tell Daddy it's a quarter to ten; tell him that Grace is waiting to have breakfast with him.

Please don't wake anybody just for me.

Grace said 'anybody' instead of Philip, for she was finding difficulty in addressing Philip and Anne by their Christian names, and until now she had solved the problem by referring to them as 'you', 'he' and 'she'.

—No you won't be disturbing him. Philip's so fond of sleeping, but he'll be angry if no one wakes him. Go on Sarah, wake Daddy.

Obediently Sarah ran upstairs and fifteen minutes later a sleepy Philip emerged, a lapsed Saturday look on his face.

—Hello. Did you sleep well?

—Yes thank you, Grace said primly.

He looked at her as if he expected her to provide details of her night's sleep. Hastily she responded,

—The bed's very comfortable.

—A polite guest, he said, smiling, waiting.

Under the persuasion of his glance she almost began, —Oh yes I slept very well thank you, I had some strange dreams, I dreamed –

—The bed was comfortable then?

—Yes thank you.

85

—When you come again, and Dad's here, you'll find the other room is more Spartan.

—Oh! Anne exclaimed suddenly, looking dismayed. —Oh! I hope you don't mind having seed potatoes in your room.

(Does parenthood bring an increased fear of things 'coming in from outside', Grace wondered.)

—I showed her the potatoes, Philip said.

—I don't mind them at all, Grace assured them – she was not so consistently inane that she added, —I *like* having seed potatoes in my room when I visit for the weekend, although she was surprised that she did not make an equally foolish remark.

Sarah and Noel had finished their breakfast. The adult gold-rush was in progress with Philip, Anne, Grace busily sifting and spooning sugar-puffs while between mouthfuls Philip was explaining that the seed potatoes were a new variety which he hoped to grow successfully.

—What is their particular characteristic? Grace asked, glowing with her manifestation of deep intelligence, remembering vaguely that when she bought potatoes she asked for 'King Edwards please', but there were other varieties, Arran Chief . . . they bred potatoes almost as they bred dogs for their particular qualities . . . didn't they? She had never bothered to find why some were called King Edward; an interesting trick of fame to have given one's name to a potato.

—I believe they taste like kumaras.

—Oh, Grace said.

Back to New Zealand. She remembered kumaras, creamy-golden and sweet, and the flax basket that old Jimmy had given their father, a special kumara basket; and their mother's talk of kumaras, her irritating allusions to them as if they belonged to a world which only their mother knew and which her children could not share: the world of the Maoris, and the Maori pa, and the old whalers and sealers in the Straits. Grace knew that although her mother had been a generous woman who would never refuse to share her possessions, she placed such a special value upon her experiences that the more she talked of them and shared them, the more she seemed to hoard them within herself, like miser's treasure, to turn them over and over, studying them, delighting in them, with her dreams curled selfishly around them.

—You've tasted kumaras?

—Oh yes, yes.

So he was going to plant a part of New Zealand in his Winchley garden. More homeland images rose in Grace's mind; deftly she seized and submerged them. Taking a page of a morning newspaper from a chair beside her she pretended to read it but was unable to absorb the words or the meaning. Sarah with a small naked doll wrapped in a piece of towelling came up to her to explain that her doll was baby Jesus. Anne lifted Noel from his pot and began to dress him like a space-man for his morning sleep in the pram on the lawn.

Except for the murmuring of children there was silence. Grace thought, Perhaps I ought to comment on some news. Unfortunately Grace was one of those people who can become a bore and an irritation to others and an anguish to themselves because their lives are dominated by 'ought'. 'What ought I to do? Do you think I ought to –' . . . They refuse to let a situation rest; they must tamper with it, adjust it, change it, impose upon it their immediate concern of 'ought'.

—I'm afraid I'm not taking in a word of this newspaper, she said, meaning her remark as an apology.

—Sarah! Anne spoke sharply. —Come away. Don't bother Grace, she wants to read the newspaper.

When Grace had said, 'I'm taking nothing in', Philip had looked at her with a small stirred expression of anxiety; she could see it in his eyes, as if some thought or feeling that lay asleep there had moved and flecks of an anxiety had risen around it, like dust.

Grace wished she had kept silent.

—I find it hard to concentrate too, Anne said enthusiastically.

—Newspapers are about all I can manage in the weekend, and then it's a struggle, Philip said in a bolstering manner.

It was almost as if, in making her remark, she had collapsed, and Philip and Anne had rushed to help her, concerned for her, anxious to explain that they too were in the habit of collapsing.

I must be careful, Grace thought, not to make another such remark.

—Terrible things are happening in South Africa, she said cheerfully, pointing to a headline.

—What things? Philip asked.

Philip and Anne lay, eyes alert, head between paws, waiting to pounce upon her words. Panicstricken, her ideas and the words which would have supported them scuttled to the sheltering foliage of incoherence.

—Oh, the usual, she said foolishly, pointing to a newspaper paragraph.

Suddenly baby Jesus was lying on her lap. She took the doll, propping its head against the leg of the table; it had no eyes; they had been scooped out and their sockets chipped like tiny chalk quarries; its belly was plump, its belly-button (the proud and only immodesty admitted by doll-manufacturers who therefore make it a field-day of anatomy) was rimmed and deep like a tiny inflatable swimming-pool; it was unsexed, but Sarah assured Grace that it was baby Jesus, a girl.

Self-consciously Grace kept it propped against the table; resisting the frightening temptation to hold it in her arms, against her breast. As children do, with their sensitive antennae probing an adult's emotions, Sarah realised Grace's desire to possess her baby Jesus. She reached forward suddenly and claimed it, putting her arms protectively around it, folding the piece of towelling against its head.

She looked directly but kindly at Grace.

—It's my baby Jesus, she said, gently challenging.

Grace looked around her with a furtive air. —I hope no one's seen this, she thought. I hope no one's reading my mind. I wish I were not so exposed; I wish it were time to sleep; it is not the night but the day that 'has a thousand eyes'. I wish —

—Do you like rice?

Already Anne was considering the preparation of lunch.

Oh yes, Grace said firmly. Anne might just as well have asked her if she liked poetry or the theatre or the country. Yes was Grace's favourite word; it saved so much explaining; it was more often when you said No that people demanded explanations, waited for you to speak, argued with you to prove that your *No* should have been *Yes*.

—Dad's funny, Anne said. She paused and looked at Philip, carefully giving him the responsibility of discussing her father's whims.

—Yes. Philip laughed. —Rice is a pudding, Dad says. He won't eat it with anything as a first course; simply refuses it. But he'll eat the same rice the next day if it's called pudding.

—Well he's never been used to it as a first course, Anne said, defending her father now that he was being criticised. —He's always thought of rice as a pudding.

She laughed gently, not complaining, merely stating in a surprised way —I have to cook special meals for Dad. He's so finicky. What is it, Grace?

—Nothing, oh nothing.

Are they talking of Anne's father? Grace said to herself. Or is it of Jimmy, my brother, and the day two years ago when he said to me,

—I can't eat egg, I've never been able to eat egg,

89

and I realised that for the thirty years or more that I had known him I had been unaware that he didn't 'eat egg'; it was not as simple a revelation as it seemed; for thirty years he must have had a secret pact with my mother, an arrangement for the cooking of special meals; why hadn't he talked about it? People enjoy talking of their dislikes in food. Once, I achieved prestige and fame within the family by 'hating pineapple'; everyone flocked for my share; until the day I decided to taste it and found I liked it and had to wage continual war against the tradition, so firmly established, that I disliked pineapple!

I wondered if there were many more important things about my brother which I did not know. I remember the dismay I felt when he said it. —I don't eat egg . . . The rebellion, jealousy; the emptiness, as if something had escaped me through my own carelessness.

—I'm sorry I missed seeing your father.

—You'll have to come again to discuss liver fluke and pulpy kidney, Philip said, smiling at Grace. She felt embarrassed, remembering the vivid note about sheep diseases which she had written to Philip in response to his invitation. Ah, if only she lived for ever in a world of correspondence, writing (she thought) daring, imaginative, witty letters that revealed nothing of her social stupidity!

—Yes, she said inadequately. —Yes, I must come again. I like it here.

Oh God.

She looked vaguely around the kitchen.

—A cigarette?

—No thank you, I don't usually smoke. Well, I will have one, thank you. I don't smoke except in company.

When she sensed that the moments, once forming a perimeter of no escape, were gradually breaking into characteristic Saturday mid-morning hyphens, she slipped out between a gap in two moments, murmured excuses, and escaped to her room. She had made her bed. She had unpacked what she needed from her bag. She had brought far too much, having deceived herself by dreams of —Have a sherry, This is my wife, Anne. Anne, this is Grace Cleave.

I saw too many films when I was a child, Grace thought. She knew that she could never escape from the influence of Saturday 'pictures' when she and her three sisters and brother straggled along to their 'shouted' treat at the Majestic or Opera House. All the wives in the 'pictures' drank sherry. Mae West drank it too. In Grace's family the invitation Have a sherry, was an invitation to take part in moral depravity.

Grace smiled to herself; her imaginative naiveté was incredible. All journalists are sophisticated, blasé, their wives cuckold them and drink sherry; their houses are American dreams; they climb – no, sink into fast red or white cars and whizz round the country roads splashing the natives with mud, tooting their horns in the narrow lanes . . .

Grace zipped her bag shut. She was ashamed that she had spent so long in trying to decide what to wear during the weekend. She had been away for the weekend only once or twice before in her life, and the last time had been an ordeal and a revelation, and Grace came home obsessed with her latest piece of knowledge about human beings – if you were a woman away for the weekend you carried a handbag with your handkerchief in it, and when you wanted to blow your nose you snipped open your bag and withdrew your handkerchief.

And Grace had never known! She always tucked her handkerchief in her sleeve and she had never carried a handbag up and down inside a house; it would look as if she did not trust anyone.

It was taking so long to get used to the ways of the world; Grace did not think she would ever learn.

91

She inspected the jersey and skirt that she had hung over the back of a chair. It's true, she said. I look like an unemployed housemaid. She had worked as a housemaid and found it a successful disguise, but now when she wanted to shed her disguise she found it had grown to be a part of her. She was so used to it that only a few days before her journey to Winchley she had been walking along Earls Court Road, and a middle-aged woman of whom she asked the way had said

—It's along here, I'm going there myself,
and in the hundred yards of their walk together the woman advised Grace, judging from her appearance, that she ought to visit a certain agency in Kensington High Street if she wanted a really good domestic job; they paid you four shillings an hour and fares, you had a modern place among rich people who, if you worked well for them, would bring you fresh eggs and cream from their weekend cottage in the country.

—You pay for the eggs and cream of course, the woman said. —But they're fresh. You take my advice and go straight to that agency in Kensington High Street.

—Thank you. I will, Grace promised.

12

Grace was feeling increasing panic at the thought of going downstairs to join the family. The longer she stayed in her room, the more afraid she became. She decided that by going for a walk she would avoid the embarrassments of trying to be sociable. Putting on her coat and headscarf, taking her gloves and her small purse, she went boldly downstairs to the kitchen.

—Grace-Cleave's going for a walk, she said, adopting Sarah's way of speaking about her.

—Do you still walk around London? Philip asked.

At her interview in London when he asked, —How do you spend your time when you're not writing, she had answered, —I walk in the streets. I walk and walk.

—Yes, I still walk.

—Very far?

—Oh, she said daringly, remembering that she had walked so far only during the bus strike, —I walk, say, from Kentish Town to Camberwell.

—Kentish Town to Camberwell!

—Oh yes.

As if it were an almost daily walk.

—Usually (she modified her boast), I walk only two or three miles.

—Dad likes walking, doesn't he Philip?

—Yes. Dad walks miles every afternoon. He's not been used to it though.

—Oh yes he has, on the farm, there's quite a bit of walking to do.

—Didn't he ride?

—Yes, but walking to inspect fences, look for sheep . . .

—But they do most of that on horseback don't they love?

—Yes. I suppose they do.

Philip gave a great guffaw.

—Dad walks chiefly for his bowels.

—Yes he does. He's so bashful about it isn't he Phil.

—I think he likes to walk, but he's thinking most of the time about his bowels.

—It gives him an interest though, Phil, doesn't it?

—Yes love.

Grace moved towards the door. Her head was dizzy with undercurrents.

In a guest-ridden tone she said,

—I'll be away a couple of hours.

Anne, now preparing to do the weekly washing, busy at the washing machine, leaned down and extracted a small wet shoe.

—Oh Phil, here's Noel's shoe. Do you think it will dry?

She turned to Grace.

—We'd thought of going into Winchley this afternoon to show you a few of the sights and change Sarah's library book. You'd like to come?

—Oh yes!

—It's a nice bright day.

—We'll be having dinner about one, Philip said, host-ridden, as Grace went out the back door. He came with her.

—Would you like a map?

—Oh yes!

He found her a map.

—Thank you very much.

He marked their street.

—You're here. The village is along there. There's the golf course.

They walked in the garden. He pointed among the shocked frosted plants to a small aged grey rosemary bush.

—We're hoping the rosemary has survived. We're rather lucky to have been able to grow it up here.

—Yes, Grace said.

He showed her the back gate and the path she would take to reach the village.

—Goodbye.

—Goodbye. Be seeing you.

Alone, outside the gate, Grace breathed relief and freedom.

13

At once she was conscious of the deceit of the weather. From inside the house, with Philip and Anne and Noel and Sarah in the kitchen, human and alive, whenever Grace had looked from the window it had seemed to her that the day would be sunny. Anne too had been deceived, for swept close in family warmth she had said, —It's such a bright promising day.

The first garish light of morning had the appearance of being softened by the wintry sun – that is, from inside the Thirkettle kitchen.

Now, alone, trying to walk on the layers of ice on the track through the park Grace looked about her at a landscape from which all life had been wrung; sodden grass; small heaps of black snow; slush; the trees standing stripped and grey as if the snowstorm, passing by like a plague of locusts, had devoured their life. Grace stamped her feet to get rid of their numbness. She walked carefully, her arms spread slightly, like wings. Up here in the north there seemed to be a draught from somewhere in the sky, as if the northern door leading to the homes of the Gods had been left open; they were the relentless Gods – Thunder, War, Revenge, Night; the wind blowing from their sky caverns was so penetrating and paralysing with its chill that Grace wanted to sink on her knees into the ice and beg for mercy. She walked on and on, shivering, her flesh demanding in vain a little charity from the weather, her mind yet revelling in the drama of this foreign hemisphere where North was a word full of menace and South promised sun and warmth. The traditional phrases of her own country – up north, down south, had no meaning in this part of the world. The combination of the two phrases – up north here, up north there, cancelled both meanings in such a way that Grace felt herself to be lost in a desert or snow-plain of reference; her mind grew chilled; yes-yes murdered no-no; day and night together were effaced . . .

————

At last she came to the small group of shops which made up the village. She could see only the usual dusty exhibits of a village store – giant packets of cigarettes, cardboard butter, rust-edged tins of peaches and pears, reduced; the button-cotton-wool clutter of a draper's; the shrivelled fruit, 'morning-fresh'. She might have been in a poorer London suburb. At least, she thought, the sky is clear of London smoke. Its light was distant and grey, and now that she had walked for over a mile the freezing air was giving its reward, pinching, slapping her skin as if its intention, so often misunderstood, were to resurrect the human race rather than entomb it in ice.

Birds too, Grace thought, remembering that she had been changed; Philomela; Procne; it was an old tradition; we must tend the myths, she thought; only in that way shall we survive. Survive, survive; the word wearied her; here, in the northern hemisphere, survival was as much a part of consciousness as food and sex and shelter, and yet it was no longer the prerogative of the north; even in the warm south it occupied their minds; would the seasons change, then; would people change – to beasts, or to birds, as she had done?

She unfolded her map of Winchley, located the village,

97

consulted her watch, and chose a street where the last building was marked heavily in black: *Industrial School.*

Why did her past life keep erupting and spilling dangerous
memories over her weekend?

Industrial School. She shivered with fear and her heart
quickened its beat. I'll walk past it, she said to herself, I'll see
the kind of place where my father so often threatened to send
Isy.

—You'll go to the Industrial School in Caversham. It's the
Industrial School for you. We'll have to send her to the
Industrial School.

It surprised Grace to remember that she had not thought of
an Industrial School as a school, and that it had been the
word *Industrial* which used to frighten her; it gave the image of
a vast hall (some connection, Grace used to think, with the
song Isy sang and which her mother said was a terrible song

> 'And when I die
> don't bury me at all,
> Just pickle my bones
> in Alco Hall')

a place filled with whirling black skeletons (like a sculptor's
'mobiles') of which *dust* was the flesh, and that being sent to
the Industrial School you were caged inside a skeleton and
forced to revolve with it in a fury of black dust until eventu-
ally your body became indistinguishable from the skeleton,
and if people visited the Hall (mother, father, aunts, uncles
from up north or down south) they wouldn't even realise you
were imprisoned there; they wouldn't be able to see you, and
if you had any voice and tried to speak to them they would
never hear you.

Grace had not associated the word 'school' with a place of
learning because experience had taught her to be suspicious

of the meaning of words. Hadn't she sung God Save our Gracious Tin, then discovered that the 'tin' was not a kerosene tin but an old man with medals and a beard? Hadn't she been forbidden to go near the magazine at the drill-hall, and then had found her mother reading a book which she described carelessly as 'The Railway *Magazine*'? After such experiences Grace knew that you had to take great care with words. Her mother had convinced her of this too. She talked of whales.

—A family of whales, kiddies, is called a *school*.

—A *school*? That's silly.

—Yes, a *school* of whales.

—A *school* of *wales*?

—Pronounce your words properly, their father had put in, for he was particular about pronunciation.

—It is *whales*.

So, preferring the unexpected meaning, for she could not bear to be taken by surprise, Grace had never revised her belief that an *Industrial School* was a group or family of black dusty skeletons revolving in a vast hall. Without question it would have been a terrible place to send Isy.

Grace remembered her fear when she used to lie in bed at night tucked up with her sleeping sisters and suddenly imagine that Isy would be seized and carried away. They would grab her arm and she would yell, as she so often did in play, —You're pulling my arm out of its socket! (Saying 'out of its socket' was usually enough to make anyone stop pulling because it brought the awe-inspiring image of your standing there holding an arm and not knowing how to return it to its socket, and with parents around and punishment in view that was an embarrassing position to be in.) Grace knew, however, that when 'they' came to take Isy to the Industrial School they would not be deterred by anything or anyone, they would keep pulling, and Isy, with her arm in or out of its

99

socket, would be imprisoned and slowly ground into black dust.

———

The village was out of sight now. Grace was on the road lead-ing to the Industrial School. She passed an isolated shop where she bought cigarettes and a bar of raisin chocolate. She passed a church, then an old people's housing estate, groups of small flats with a communal room facing the street. Through the floor-to-ceiling windows Grace could see a group of men and women sitting in armchairs looking from the window at the street, the people, and the occasional traffic. Although the motive in providing the large windows had been to bring the old people in contact with the life of the street, when Grace stared through at them, realising that no part of their sitting room was hidden from the public gaze, she knew a feeling of desolation, and the sordid persistence of truth which, by a thoughtful misdirection of architecture, had given the flat-dwellers the unusual characteristic of seeming to be what, in fact, they were: they had not the appearance of sitting happily in a bright common room, knitting, or reading or staring out of the windows at the interesting view: they seemed more like clients in a travel agency, passengers at a bus station, waiting to be despatched; one could imagine scattered on the low tables which helped to give the 'contemporary' look to the room, the bright brochures, the illustrated enticements fea-turing the unknown tomorrow. At least, Grace thought, there will be an endlessness of time, not the calculated so many days so many guineas, and no Morning Free, Afternoon Sightseeing.

How dare I? she said to herself. They are happy. They like to see the world outside. They have no wish to be shut within dark brick walls in rooms with small high windows. It is just that when age waits so obviously to book a ticket to the world of the dead it offends my sensibility; perhaps they (they, they, they) are wise enough to enjoy it; travel agencies, bus stations are interesting places; it sharpens the mind, enriches the heart to haunt areas of arrival and departure.

Grace found that she could always dismiss a disturbing thought by wrapping it in a platitude.

The Industrial School was near. She felt her heart thudding. She felt afraid. To see an Industrial School after all those years of vulnerable childhood when grownups could threaten and punish and one's world loomed with frightening images of 'truant officer' 'welfare officer' 'health inspector' 'Industrial School' 'Borstal'! For a moment Grace's courage failed her. She had a wild idea that as she passed the school she would be seized, dragged inside, kept a prisoner for ever. Had that been where Isy had really gone, in the end, after she died? She had thought about it at times. —She's with God, their mother had said, and had made a great fuss about what it would be like meeting her again on Resurrection Day, although she had irritatingly refused to acknowledge or explain the difficulties of a Resurrection Day reunion. There had to be room to resurrect, there had to be means of recognition – it was no use carrying their father's joking symbol of recognition – 'a white-handled pocketknife in a lefthand waistcoat pocket'. There were discrepancies of age, too . . . Grace had been sure it would not work, it would never work, there would have to be some other arrangement made.

She had not been so sure, then, about Isy's whereabouts. It was all very well to be 'with God' but it was a vague locality which described nowhere, and Grace had known that when her mother was faced with difficult questions which had frightening answers she was apt to reply vaguely. People going 'away' were often revealed to be dead. 'Holidays' were prison. 'Nervous breakdowns' were madness, thinking you were the

King of the Solomon Islanders. Grace learned so early the deceptions of words that she regarded every statement with suspicion. 'With God' indeed! Where else would Isy be when she had been threatened so often with the Industrial School? Where else but at the Industrial School?

It was almost twelve o'clock. The faint blue light in the sky had disappeared. The world was depressingly grey. An ice-edged wind had sprung from the moor and was shuffling the old brittle leaves along the pavement and so transforming the air that it seemed on the verge of turning to ice. Grace found breathing an effort. She slowed her footsteps to gather courage before she arrived at the Industrial School. Again she consulted the map, compared it with her own position in the street. Yes, the Industrial School should be here, here, she said firmly, turning her eyes bravely to the right. There was no Industrial School. Again she consulted the map, making sure of her position. Again she looked about her; there was no Industrial School.

It's an old map, yes, it's an old map, she said, shivering. The sun had gone. Am I dreaming? she said to herself. She imagined the conversation when she returned to the Thirkettle house,

—Where did you walk?

—I walked to the Industrial School.

They would look at her in bewilderment. —Industrial School?

But it was here, printed on the map, labelled, with the buildings heavily outlined in black.

Procne. Philomela. The summer swallow. 'So perish the old Gods but out of the sea of time –'

Her father, who was always impatient with Gods, would have shouted at this Northern sky, —It's a freezing-chamber in here, Can't you shut the blasted door!

Grace turned up her coat-collar and walked slowly back towards Holly Road.

How had she ever become used to living in Great Britain, she wondered. How had she ever been able to exchange the sun, the beach, the shimmering tent of light, the dramatic land-scape, mountains, rivers, gullies, glaciers, for the brick bleeding wound that seemed so much a part of this country; for the spindly winter trees, so tired, growing out of the squalor, as if a slovenly god, leaning down to try to clean the wound, had seized a few twigs to probe it, and amused by the sight, had left them sticking out of the wound. Great Britain was so full of waste paper, sooty paper, bus tickets, bus tickets – once when Grace was alighting from a bus and dutifully put-ting her used ticket in the 'receptacle provided' she had been too energetic and before she realised what was happening she had emptied the bin over the steps of the bus and into the road; a snowstorm of tickets with Grace Cleave, apologising as usual, marooned in it. It was a dismal grey wintry land with too many people; it was people who made the squalor; if you must have snow let it be out of sight of the human race; no; for every contamination there is a poem.

She came to the park. The poverty of the north made her feel near to weeping; it was not material poverty, not lack of money or work, but the drab world and its poor supply of sun and warmth; people in Winchley would never sit drinking wine at little tables under the sky; when rich times came again (and why should they not?) they would banquet in vast north-ern halls, sipping from goblets of poison, and surviving it.

———

She had almost reached the street when a woman emerged from one of the terraced houses facing the park. Her dress was patched in black and white, outlined sharply against the grey day. To Grace's astonishment the woman suddenly flapped her arms then opening her mouth she screeched three times and then was silent. Then she began screeching again. Grace stared at her black and white patched dress, listened to the screeching, and thought, —She's a magpie, she's not a woman, she's a bird. As she watched the woman more closely she saw the final change taking place in her – she had surprised her in private metamorphosis – she saw the arms mould themselves to wings, the black and white patched dress change to feathers about her body, her nose extend sharply to form a beak. There was no need for her voice to change. She began screeching once more; she was calling someone, her children. She flapped her wings belligerently as Grace passed her, she turned her bright fierce eyes towards her, then she dropped one wing limply at her side and fluttering the other as if clearing an obstacle from the air, she resumed her screeching.

No, it's not the call of the magpie, Grace considered. Perhaps she is a marsh bird; a plover, peewit; why should I see her here, now? Does she know that I too have changed to a bird? That it is time for me to fly towards another summer?

—See anything interesting on your walk?

—I was walking in the park when I saw a woman changed to a bird –

Why should she not speak the truth at least once in her life? The need to tell Philip and Anne, to stand in the big untidy kitchen and say, aloud, I saw a woman change to a bird, was so desperate that Grace did not know how she would be able to prevent herself from telling. She knew there would be embarrassing consequences. Hasty Reassurances. The subject switched to one more harmless. Her limited social experience made her feel certain of the response to her news; she did not question the accuracy of her forecast, although she knew she was being unfair to Philip and Anne. Perhaps for the first time in her life she was among people whose imagination was not housed in a small dark room with no windows, whose understanding and sympathy were liberal, adventurous.

Why not tell them, why not explain? she said to herself. I don't wish to inhabit the human world under false pretences. I'm relieved to have discovered my identity after being so confused about it for so many years. Why should people be afraid if I confide in them? Yet people will always be afraid and jealous of those who finally establish their identity; it leads them to consider their own, to seclude it, cosset it, for fear it may be borrowed or interfered with, and when they are in the act of protecting it they suffer the shock of realising that their identity is nothing, it is something they dreamed and never knew; and then begins the painstaking search – what shall they choose – beast? another human being? insect? bird?

If I confide that I have become a bird, others may want to change in the same way; or the shock may be so great that even Philip and Anne, who have qualities of mind to deal with unexpected situations, may not be able to adapt them-selves in time, to accept the truth of my identity. The strain of constant adaptation to so many fearful events and discoveries is already too much to bear with sanity; one has to keep pre-tending to slip successfully into the new mould; a time will come when the tailored and camouflaged mind breaks beneath the burden; the stick insect in our brains no longer cares to resemble a twig on the same habitual human tree in the mere hope that it may survive extinction.

14

Walking slowly because she was still too early for lunch and she dreaded the extra half-hour of conversation, Grace at last came to Holly Road and the Thirkettles' house. She knocked lightly on the back door and went in.

—Hello. Had a good walk?

—Yes thank you.

—I'm just getting the lunch ready.

Anne's face was flushed with the heat of the stove and the cooking and with feeding and calming Noel and Sarah who were both claiming attention from Philip. He sat on one chair with his feet on another and Sarah was crouched on his knees, her hands in his, being pulled to and fro.

Grace laughed unexpectedly and happily.

—That's trolley works, she said, and instantly regretted saying it; they would ask her to explain.

Philip was looking attentively at her, waiting. Anne paused in her serving of the meal to listen. Grace felt trapped.

—Yes, she said clumsily —that, I mean the way you and Sarah are holding hands like that and pulling . . . that's trolley works . . .

Still they waited for an explanation. A deep despair filled Grace's mind as she watched Philip, Anne, Noel, Sarah, so far away, wanting to understand her language, in this case an ordinary family word – surely they themselves had a family language which they would find difficult to explain to others! What if she were to turn towards Anne and say, smiling, —How like Shelley's first wife you are!

Anne would not realise the significance. How often Grace and her sisters had exclaimed to one another, —I'm getting to be like Shelley's wife, you're like Shelley's wife! Meaning that the material vain affairs of the world were intruding on their imaginative concerns; remembering, from a shared reading of the life of Shelley, that he had complained of Harriet, —When I'm thinking of poetry she's thinking of buying hats!

—Trolley works?

Grace longed to lean her head on the table and weep and weep, her mouth felt dry.

—Trolley works, she repeated. —We used to play like that, as if we were trolleys on the railway, you know how the gangers work the trolleys?

Gangers, trolleys: they did not understand her railway vocabulary.

—Yes, the gangers were always going up and down in their trolleys. When we were children the area near the railway was our playground – the engine sheds, goods sheds, the piles of sleepers, the old turntables, disused huts . . .

Philip's eyes showed a worried expression and when he spoke she was dismayed to realise that he seemed to regard her as a small child who is playing near the railway line and in danger of being killed by the trains,

—But it's dangerous for you to play near the railway line, he said sharply.

There was a note in his voice which said, —You mustn't do it again, understand? What on earth are your parents thinking of to let you play near the trains?

Feeling at once proud, bold, orphaned, in need of being 'taken into care', Grace said innocently,

—I suppose it was a risk. We didn't think about it at the time.

Philip looked sternly at her, as if to say, —Don't play there again!

Chastened, but pleased that his concern for her reached so far backwards in time, Grace made scraping movements with her chair, in response to the scraping movements the others were making, drawing their chairs to the table for the meal.

—The sun's gone, Anne said. —We'll go into Winchley as soon as we've had lunch.

—Anything interesting on your walk?

—I saw an old people's housing estate. I didn't like it. Like a travel agency with the old people waiting to be despatched.

—Well they are, aren't they?

Philip's mind was so clear. He could walk the straight white line from beginning to end without stumbling.

—Yes, perhaps they are.

Then trying to sound calm, Grace said,

—Isn't there an Industrial School somewhere near?

—Industrial School? I don't know of any. Why?

—I thought I saw one on the map.

She wanted to say —Do you know about Industrial Schools, how you can be sent there for disobeying or poking a face at your father or stealing or not coming when you're called or playing with boys in the plantations, I mean the pine plantations where they've been felling the trees and they're still lying covered with pine-needles and there are corker places there, only I mustn't say 'corker' because Mrs Biddy says it, she's always saying it, and I get tired of saying words which other people are always using. When I say 'corker' I'm irritated with myself and my mother says quite sharply, —You're like Mrs Biddy saying that word over and over. Say something different. You don't know Mrs Biddy, do you, Philip and Anne? She used to live over the road with her husband who was a ganger

(ganger, trolley, turntable, engine-shed), but they 'shifted' down south, and their eldest daughter was married and came to our place for a honeymoon and we giggled and giggled and followed the couple everywhere, waiting for them to do it, and for us to watch, and they went home sooner than they'd expected, but they're quite old now, and though you might think I'm still a child in danger from the trains, I'm quite old too, I've *mellowed*, everyone's *mellowed*, the human race turns at last into a tree of ripe pears. What a fate! And to think that we were worried over our survival!

—There *may* be an Industrial School near. The map is out-of-date, I think.

Noticing Anne's flushed face and the special care she was taking with serving the meal, Grace thought, Now is the time to praise her cooking.

—I like this pie very much.

—Do you? I didn't make the pastry myself. It's packet pastry.

—The people at the flat left some packet pastry. I can't manage to bake it. This is so light and tasty.

—It's only steak and kidney, Anne said, pleased, yet determined not to accept more praise than she felt was due. —I bought it yesterday at the butcher's. The woman in front of me (what do you think of these English queues?) was buying some too, and we agreed it looked worth buying. 'I think I'll get some,' I said to the woman. 'I don't often buy it,' she told me, 'but I can't resist it today. My dog will love it. This shop is quite good for dog-meat . . .' —You know, Anne said, —the English and their dogs!

Her voice showed a strong New Zealand accent. There was general laughter, Sarah joining in and exclaiming, —The English and their dogs!

—You're a little hybrid, aren't you? Philip said fondly. —You're English and New Zealand.

He turned to Grace,

—We're going again this year to the far North-West of Scotland. It's wild, remote, it's as like the West Coast of New Zealand as any place I've seen. You know the West Coast?

—No.

Grace remembered, ashamed, that when Philip sent her a card from Scotland she had answered with knowing references to 'the wild wet West Coast of New Zealand', and now she had to confess that she'd never seen it!

—I met Anne there. I was baching and got invited to an evening at Tim's house (you'll know Tim) and Anne was there. She saw me and went for her life to grab me, and she got me.

It was the usual half-joking explanation of courtship and marriage, which Philip contrived to sound complimentary to Anne, who instead of looking with a bridled resentment, smiled fondly at him, lovingly establishing his identity, instinctively fulfilling the true purpose of love, that is, courageously to place the loved one apart from oneself. Union is strength – the strength to acknowledge that one is two; supported by love any tissue-paper identity may stand like stone.

High in the sky, buffeted by the winds from everywhere, trying to persist in her course of flight as a migratory bird, Grace felt the need for a warm supporting wind blowing in her direction. Yet she was not envious of Philip and Anne; she felt pleased and satisfied at the certainty of their love. She was interested that Philip had so arranged his life that he seemed to live for ever, in work and play, on the 'wild wet West Coast of New Zealand'. At the interview in London he had remarked,

—I feel more nostalgic for New Zealand than Anne does.

He was saying it now!

—I'd like to go back there; it's an exciting, young country, full of ideas . . .

Anne laughed gently,

—Do you know, he used to be so disgusted with the place that every night he played Bach on the gramophone to console himself.

—I admit that, Philip said. —Now that the old identities are dying, those West Coast towns have a nothingness that is quite frightening. There are fewer interesting people.

—You met me there!

—Oh, you're different. You're an exceptional member of the human race!

Grace was surprised that Philip did not leave his remark as a natural, expected compliment. No sooner had he made it than he looked uneasy, and with careful, almost frightening accuracy, he began to qualify it. —No, of course you're not an exceptional member of the human race; you're human, like anyone else, no more, no less . . .

How strange, Grace thought. Being human seems to mean so much; being *normally* human, if such a state can be discovered and recorded. She wondered at the source of the momentary fear in Philip's eyes as he heard his compliment spoken aloud and hastened to retract it; perhaps, after all, it was merely the journalist's passion for the truthful statement?

What would Philip and Anne say, Grace thought, if I confessed that I am a migratory bird? It is likely that they would turn upon me and kill me. When Philip talks of the West Coast there is an apprehension deep in his eyes: I *know*. Isn't it there, in the south, that they have discovered the flightless bird, the takahe, long thought to be extinct? Is there a fear that it will flourish and increase, 'take over' the sparsely populated country? Why is so much fiction preoccupied with the conquest of the human race by birds, vegetation, insects, visitors from outer or inner space? Why is a sensitive intelligent husband like Philip so aware of the common threat that he cannot make an ordinary remark to his wife without being perturbed by its underlying dreadful seriousness?

—You know there was a bird discovered recently on the West Coast. The takahe. It was thought to be extinct.

Grace shivered. Why did Philip say that, at this moment? Was there, after all, some communication on this weekend of platitudinous I like your cooking, You're good with the children, yes I like Winchley?

The word 'extinct' had always been, to Grace, one imbued with an emotion different from the personal unhappiness aroused by the word 'death'. It was curious that 'extinct' had been a favourite word used by Grace's mother who had seemed, in some way, to be in touch with the past, to be able to reach and shake its trees till the fruit of yesterday dropped in her lap: those groves of shadowy trees like the underground orchard where the boughs were silver and the fruit was gold and a branch separated from its parent bough gave forth a sighing sound like plaintive horn music; all those groves of trees, the branches filled with birds, now extinct, and the mammoths like out-of-date Victorian furniture, stumbling through the undergrowth, their tiny dim eyes like drawer-knobs; the poor bric-a-brac of the animal world . . .

—They're *extinct* now, Grace's mother used to say. Extinction was the fate of animals and birds and insects, seldom of people. And what a fascination lay in the tuatara house at the Zoo! Crowds gazing at the tuatara waiting for it to show signs of life; gazing and thinking, we're alive, you *may* become *extinct*. Most of the animals and birds known by you are *extinct*. Yet is there not envy, too, in their gazing? —What was it like, tuatara? Why don't you speak to us, why don't you *tell, explain*?

Then, resentful of the silence,

—Who cares about you, anyway? Who bothered to save you? Why were you saved?

—Yes, Grace said. —The takahe was believed to be *extinct*.

She emphasised the word. What a clear final sound it had! How wonderful to be able to dismiss a species in one word! One hoped that the word would keep its place among animals and birds but one never knew with words . . . remember magazine, sleeper, school, and the kerosene tin for which the nation sang its prayer?

15

They drank their coffee. It was almost three o'clock. The day was darkening swiftly and already the frost was pressing its sucker-fingers upon the windowpanes. After-dinner comfort could not erode the determination of Philip and Anne to carry out their promise to show Grace Winchley and to change Sarah's library book.

—You don't mind going to Winchley?

—I think it will be very pleasant.

(After all, Grace thought, they may be longing to go to Winchley.)

—We'll have to hurry. The market closes early. We wanted to show you the market. And there's Sarah's library book. You're sure you'd like to go?

Do they mean me to say Yes or No, Grace wondered. I have no social intuition. I'm not used to dancing around invitations simply to make a pretty pattern of No's and Yes's. I'd like to go to Winchley. But the day's grown colder and darker and we've just had a meal and everyone's feeling lazy; but they've promised, and they can't go back on their promise and – who knows? – extraordinary pleasures may be waiting in Winchley.

Grace joined in the general excitement of people getting ready for an expedition. While Anne dressed the children and Philip found his coat Grace went upstairs for her boots, coat and headscarf, and when she came down to the kitchen everyone was waiting ready to burst from the door in excitement.

They went outside. They looked at one another, shrank into their warm coats, turned up their collars, pulled their gloves more tightly about their wrists. Already the children's noses were glistening and their screwed-up little faces were blue with cold. Noel began to whimper.

—We're going to Winchley, Noel, Anne said brightly. —We're going to show Grace the market and change Sarah's library book.

They waited for the bus. There was no pretence now about the weather, no cheerful reminder that the sun had promised to shine, only a tacit admission that promises are strictly for people and that the weather has no conscience about the survival or extinction of the human race. Standing, all shivering now, their shoulders bowed, they might have been naked, their clothes seemed to provide so little warmth. The two children had an aged appearance, as if they had strayed from the pages of *Jude*; their next move, Grace considered, might be frightful, they were so exposed to the merciless judgment of the weather. The melodramatic 'Done because we were too many' seemed not unimaginable.

As the bus drew near Anne took Sarah, while Philip lifted Noel from the push-chair.

—Will you take Noel, Grace?

Grace took Noel in her arms, careful to hold him the correct way, to show anyone who happened to see, that she was used to small children. She was so careful with him, her arm was arranged just so tucked under his bottom, while his head leaned over her shoulder, and just for a moment Philip and Grace were husband and wife taking their little boy (how like his father!) on the bus to Winchley. With a lightning snatch, like a goldfish after its food, Grace seized the swimming moment and was not disturbed by her greed in sharing it with no one for she was calmly and thankfully aware that Philip had no desire to feed upon it.

He took Noel in his arms once again.

—Thank you, Grace.

Her face burned. She took her handkerchief from her cardigan sleeve and blew her nose. Anne and Sarah came drifting towards them like islands separated from the mainland; then, as a family continent harbouring a migratory castaway, they climbed on the bus, travelled ten minutes, and arrived at Winchley.

—Our first call is at the library, then the market, Philip said with determination, using his words and their certainty as part of a campaign against the bitter cold. There seemed nowhere to escape from the snowfilled sootfilled wind. It blew upon their skin as if their outer layer of skin had been peeled away leaving a raw rasping wound spread over their body. They struggled along the grey streets in a bizarre enactment of an Arctic expedition which could have been recorded in the usual dramatic diary – 'Supply of warmth diminishing; hope to reach library and market by five-thirty; hopes failing . . .' Grace would not have been surprised if Philip had suddenly stopped and said, with a stricken look on his face, 'I'm going a while. I may be some time . . .'

They reached the library. Anne changed Sarah's book while Sarah watched, dismayed, as the seaside book where the animals had been picnicking on the sands, eating tomato sandwiches, ice cream and bananas, disappeared over the desk, and when the new book was found for her she looked suspiciously at it.

—Where's my animal book? Where's the picnic at the seaside? Mummy, Mummy, Sarah began to cry in despair.

Noel began to cry in sympathy.

Anne explained that the animals had been in a library book, to be shared with other children, and now Sarah had a new book with different animals and people in it.

—But will they be at home when we get home? They were at home today.

Noel began to wail.

—It's the cold, Philip said, playing the role of the embarrassed husband. —We'll hurry to the market. It'll be warm there.

The market was warm with bodies, steam, sweat, smells. The little group straggled along the rows of stalls. They passed a stall hung with flashy jewellery and knick-knacks where a young man and woman were standing, staring at a chocolate-box picture.

—Ooh, cooed the woman, isn't it lovely?

—It's twenty-eight bob, the man said, and drew her away.

—Did you hear that? Philip said to Grace.

She laughed. —Yes.

—Beautiful jewellery, Philip said laughing.

—Wonderful, Grace agreed, with a brazen air of – I like flashy things, you know, I appreciate this market!

They stopped at a stall displaying household furnishings and dress materials.

—I wonder, Anne said, in a meditative voice, —if they have any sheeting.

Clearly, she said this on the sudden wave of a domestic dream. Philip said quickly in a tone of mild disapproval,

—Not now, surely, love!

Anne looked slightly ashamed, but persisted. —I thought I might get some sheeting while we're here.

—Another day, Philip said, embarrassed at the sudden absorption in domestic matters.

Rejoicing, apart, Grace felt as complete and shimmering as

a mermaid. She felt sorry for Anne. She guessed that Anne might not have another chance during the week to buy the 'sheeting', that children, house and home (and *Ulysses*) would be taking all her time; when her father returned from Edinburgh and the extra meals began again, there would be no time at all to saunter into Winchley to buy a length of sheeting.

Anne's eyes were clouded with what could only be described as domestic concern: instinctive concern, like the look in the eye of a bird when it sees a stick or length of straw that could be used for its nest.

With conscious good humour Philip gently drew Anne away from the stall of household furnishings and steered them all from the warm market into the freezing air. Even in the half-hour they had been in the market, the sky had darkened; people were hurrying; the streets were busier.

—Time to go home. But first I'll show Grace the viaduct.

—Yes, Anne said loyally, —You must see the viaduct.

Grace burned with guilt; she saw Anne casting backward glances at the market and the vanished sheeting.

—Today's the kind of day to see it, Philip said.

—I think, Anne said boldly, her eyes glowing with warmth as she looked at Philip, —I'll buy some Parmesan while you show Grace the viaduct.

—All right, love.

———

—There. There's the Winchley Viaduct.

Grace looked at the viaduct. What could she say about it?

—Yes. M-m-m-m-m, she said, making a stupid noise as if she were eating cake. She cleared her throat, and stared, trying to put an intelligent expression on her face, as if she were 'taking in the effect'.

—I'm not boring you, showing you this?

—Oh no, of course not. I find it most interesting.

She slummed, as usual, in her choice of spoken words; either too many words to an idea or not enough furniture for the idea itself or somebody else's furniture; always a muddle and clutter of speech.

—What are you thinking about?

Grace did not answer. To herself she said, Tease is the operative word. Archways and eternity. 'Thou cold pastoral dost *tease* us out of thought as dost eternity.' 'All experience is an arch wherethrough gleams that untravelled world.'

My parrot memory, my self-consciousness, I'm thinking about nothing, about mathematics and the nth power, the ability to count one two three four five until, at n, the tongue swells in the mouth the syllables explode, one can only stammer n n n, the archway, any archway, you did not bring me to Winchley to pronounce eternity, spare me, you say, the pretension, do you know, you will say, you're wearing the weekend quite well, it becomes you, but your pretension is showing.

Grace thought, You care about buildings, don't you, Philip? The vegetation and geomorphology of the city: natural growths, outcrops of human flesh and spirit, corns, cancers, stone prayers, domes like institutional chamberpots or solitary breasts or cupped hands retaining the vision; these buildings are sighs, statements, denials . . . the sky like a grey handkerchief over the dead stone faces . . . I have a passion for the sunlight of memory. I'm a migratory bird, Philip. As a bird with a pathway in space I too have a special feeling for buildings, and a terror of them. Do not laugh at me. You have a lonely human courage, you know that man as well as buildings must learn to stand upright . . . do you know how brave human beings are to be walking on the earth, to be standing buffeted by weather and time and space; always the object of attack, still surviving; how can man dare to plant himself so, and then to know the magnificence of spirit which urges him to build a structure which is more than four walls and a roof . . . how can man dare? It is a marvel that he does not build his little hut, go in, shut and bolt the door, and spend his life there with his head bowed in humility. There is talk of voyaging in space, of the courage it needs – see the handsome cheerful intelligent men who have been chosen to circle the earth. It takes tremendous courage to make any encounter with inner or outer space, to walk upright, to move unsupported, seized by weather attended by time the cosmetic artist in reverse – snipping hair, writing wrinkles, padding the belly with pillows of fat . . . where does man find the courage?

In my condition as a migratory bird flying towards another summer, I find all buildings are obstacles. I must change my course when I approach them. They play tricks with sun and shadow. When I fly against them I fall stunned, my mind is confused. I have no fists now, only wings to strike at the buildings which stand in my path.

I'm a migratory bird, Philip. Shall I speak it aloud? Shall I tell Anne, Sarah, Noel?

—What are you thinking?

Philip waited for her to speak. He and Anne had expected that Grace Cleave would have ideas to express.

Grace looked silently, mournfully at him and turned to stare once again at the Winchley Viaduct, the local landmark. How complicated, interfering and insistent a local landmark may be! In the cunning everlasting ritual of identification one cannot say, pointing to oneself, boring one's guest,

—This is me, or I, I am myself. Here I am, see, I, me, myself . . . But one can say, Our town has a special landmark. Like to see it? I'll show it to you. A long interesting drive, afternoon tea somewhere, ah there's the castle, statue, scene of the crime, This is it, see it, There it is, see, there.

—You like the Viaduct then? You find it interesting?

—Yes. I see what you mean, that it is best in this light.

Grace sneezed and blew her nose.

—The north's a grim place she said finally.

———

They went down the street to the bus terminus where Anne and the children were waiting. Noel was asleep. Anne's face was rosy with cold. They talked of getting a taxi back to Holly Road but they decided against it and Grace remembered, ashamed, that Philip had brought her from the station at Relham in a taxi. A Winchley bus surged out of the muffling mist and frost. They climbed on, but this time Philip managed without asking Grace to carry Noel, although she bustled here and there offering to hold this and that —Shall I? Can I? No thanks, all the same, no it's all right thank you.

Sometimes Grace thought that *No thank you* was the most chilling phrase in the language.

When they reached Holly Road they almost ran to get to the house. In a burst of boyish gaiety Philip said, —I'll go ahead to light the fire and I'll have glasses of hot rum poured out, waiting.

He went ahead towards the house.

Cheered, they followed quickly and excitedly; it was all right after all, soon they would be home and warm. Philip had painted such a cosy picture of their homecoming that Grace, looking for the glasses of piping hot rum and the blazing fire, felt disappointed and depressed when she realised that Philip had been joking.

—Well what do you think of Winchley? Anne said as they entered the cold kitchen.

They drank coffee and smoked. The fire was out.

While Philip played with the children Anne prepared the tea. Although Grace longed to be alone in her room she stayed in the kitchen, spellbound by its returning warmth and comfort; listening to Philip and Anne, watching them, considering them, more relieved by their happiness than jealous of it, feeling herself in a gratifying way included in it. She smoked cigarettes from the two packets she had bought in the village and put on the mantelpiece for anyone's use, as her rehearsal of 'I've bought some cigarettes, Help yourself, smoke mine for a change' had been futile, she had been too shy to speak; therefore she endured Philip's surprised amused glance as (so he thought, unaware of her secret gift) she chainsmoked, without by your leave, from the family Nelsons.

—I never smoke, really, Grace said. —But I've decided to smoke this weekend.

She almost added, for Philip's benefit, —I bought these cigarettes this morning. Help yourself.

She wished she could summon courage to leave the kitchen, but her desire to stay was too strong; it seemed to her that she was at home, experiencing a peace that her own home had never provided. As she watched Anne going about her task of preparing tea (she had refused the help mechanically offered by Grace), Grace had a strange feeling that Anne was her mother, about to 'dish up' for the family, and that she was a child sitting at the big wooden table on the long kauri form which her father and his brothers and sisters had used, when they were children, as a canoe, turning it upside down and paddling it through makebelieve swift waters. Grace had never liked sitting on the form. As it was against the wall you had to creep under the table to reach it, and once there, with brother or sister beside you, you had no means of escape. If Grace tried to escape by walking along the form the flypapers hanging from the ceiling tangled in her frizzy hair and she heard the desperate buzz of trapped flies, quite unlike the usual dispersed sound a fly made in its free movement around the kitchen. It was the same frantic buzzing of a fly trapped in a spiderweb – Grace *knew*, for she and her sisters, from time to time, would say suddenly, —Let's catch flies and feed them to spiders. They would catch the fly in an old bottle or jam-jar, carry it to the spiderweb, and let it free to fly into the web – z-z-z-z-z its wings beat, the frail web shook violently, twanged like a silk bridge with an army crossing it; then a dark hairy face with lamplit eyes looked out from the hiding-place in the corner, and ascertaining that everything was ready, arranged according to providence, and goose-stepping on the silver silk tight-rope, the spider approached the fly, wrapped him neatly in a cobweb blanket until his wings no longer struggled, then drew him along the shaking web to his lair, to add him to the collection of flies' feet and strips of wing littered in his secret room.

As Grace sat in the Thirkettles' kitchen she heard again the desperate buzzing of flies trapped in her hair. She shook her head. It was always a time of panic when things were trapped in her hair. No one knew, no one knew how terrible it was to have such hair, so much of it, so curly and frizzy that it hurt to be combed, and people in the street stopped to stare at it, —Look at that girl with the hair!

Grace shook her head suddenly. Her ears buzzed with trapped blowflies, the frightening dark-blue kind, the same colour as the end slab in a small box of paints which someone gave as a Christmas or birthday present. Inside the lid were milky blue-white compartments, but the share of each colour was so small, such a thin strip on a shallow bed, that the blowfly colour was painted entirely away in one picture's thunder-filled sky.

Looking at Anne, Grace almost leaned forward to say,

—Bed 'n' syp, Mum, bed 'n' syp!

—Can't you see your mother's occupied?

Occupied. Her father always chose a long word, if he could

find one. Of the books on the bookshelf – the set of Oscar Wilde bought at a sale-room, school textbooks, old reading books of American Civil War stories, Dr Chase's *Book of Hints and Recipes* (in which the family births, marriages and deaths were recorded), a novel with a grey and white striped cover and a crippled back, called *To Pay the Price*, and God's Book, a Christadelphian manual with big print and misty lurid pictures of angels, Armageddon, and again, the mechanically impossible Resurrection Day – the red-bound dictionary was most used, especially by Grace's father who attempted all the word-puzzles he could find. Grace used to try to help him. She remembered once spending the whole evening in search of a word of six letters, and the more elusive the word seemed, the more determined her father became to discover it; everyone had gone to bed when he was still searching for the word. Grace went to bed when she couldn't keep awake any longer. The next day or the day after her father said suddenly, —It's *rattan*, it's *rattan*. For all his triumph he might have won the Melbourne Cup!

Her father liked to regard himself as the literate member of the family. He was the Railway Union Secretary, and beneath business notes he signed his name, with a flourish, followed by *Union Sec.*

—Bed 'n' syp, Mum, Bed 'n' syp!

Her mother was reciting poetry, her own verse,

> 'He was a poet, he loved the wild thunder
> as it crashed in the universe; now he sleeps under,
> under the grass he loved; stilled now his hand.
> Only a poet's heart could understand.'

The poet, of course, was Grace's mother, who, whether through the family poverty or her own conviction of the working of a poet's mind, insisted that the best poems were always written on the backs of envelopes, on scraps of letters.

She had evidence to prove it. She spoke of So-and-So who wrote his masterpiece on a bill that he couldn't pay; to Grace's mother this seemed the most powerful and effective revenge against poverty.

—Oh, please Mum, bed 'n' syp!

Suddenly Grace's father began to shout.

—Haven't I told you before . . . everything I say goes in one ear and out the other . . .

Startled, Grace turned to look at Philip, who, if Anne were playing the part of Mother, should have changed to Father. He hadn't changed at all, he was Philip wearing his weekend clothes, the relaxed professional man playing with his children; with just a small spot of tired darkness like a tiny black hailstone or punctuation mark set deep in his gold-flecked eyes.

———

I wonder, Grace thought. I'm glad I'm not like those dress-maker's dummies whose heads are built in the shape of a cage, or my thoughts would fly out through the bars. But I must know, I *must know* the reason for the strangeness of this week-end.

Philip is interested in architecture. Their love has an architectural quality but I feel that it is not yet complete; the foundations are strong, there are walls and roof enough to give shelter from the storm; Philip is a serious builder who has taken great care to set up a firm scaffold. A scaffold? A maga-zine? A School? There's a shape hanging from the scaffold, a small boy in a blue woollen cap like a USA baseball cap; he is stiff and dead; it is Noel. How like Philip he is, the clean intellectual shining beneath the beggar-boy snot!

But it is not Philip's and Anne's house of love that I am seeing, it is a real house, the one from Edendale, being rebuilt in Glenham, and we are living temporarily in the huts and it is snowing. There aren't enough hankies to go round, the air is clouded with Friar's Balsam, the Dunedin aunt with the goitre is saying,

—She's delirious, she's delirious,
and I'm crying because my legs ache and ache. Growing pains. Is growing so terrible? And what was that my mother said about the little boy at Outram who 'grew too fast', that he 'outgrew his strength'? Didn't he become ill and die? Is that a punishment for growing? And why do they all tease me with my mop of hair, saying that I'm like Topsy, and asking about where I was born, and I reply, knowing that they expect it,

> 'I'm the girl that never was born,
> p'ras I grew up among the corn.
> Golly, ain't I wicked!'

———

—Do you like cheese on toast?

Whenever Anne made such an enquiry Grace replied by gurgling enthusiastically, —Oh anything, anything, I eat anything.

Now, after having answered thus at the beginning of each weekend meal Grace, trying not to be so impolite and ambiguous, said —Yes, I do like cheese on toast.

She wanted to say, —My brother doesn't eat egg, he's never been able to eat egg, and I never knew.

She looked at Philip, remembering that at one spare moment in the weekend when Philip had been out of the room, Anne had said, in a confiding voice, —Philip loves *Spaghetti Bolognaise*; he'd be happy if I served *Spaghetti Bolognaise* at every meal!

Now, Grace looked wonderingly at Philip, marvelling at the quality in human beings which endows a simple commonplace like or dislike with such mystery and magic. He likes *Spaghetti Bolognaise*, she said to herself, treasuring her knowledge.

—I've enjoyed your cooking so much.

Grace felt proud to have said that. She admired Anne's conjuring ability, for although meal seemed to follow meal, and there were continual preparations, with Anne moving back and forth from sink to stove to sink to table, all was accomplished in such secrecy that if you had stopped Anne at any moment you would not have surprised her with a clod of dough in her hands or a half-peeled potato. The deliberate or unintentional way in which she concealed the preparing and cooking of the meal reminded Grace of the creation of a work of art; yet the final delivery of the food was not made in self-conscious triumph. An artist could learn from her, Grace thought. She knows how to make, to give, without the quali-fying — *It's mine.*

So often in Grace's home the food had been prepared as a love- or peace-offering, with her mother flying to the girdle to bring forth the calming pikelets, or rushing the date scones into the oven in order that the family might enjoy a few moments of hot buttered forgetfulness; or with morning stern-ness, accentuating the struggle for survival after the long unconsciousness of night and sleep, their mother, ignoring their chants of

'Eat and grow fat,
grow fat and be laughed at!'

would thrust their breakfast before them, —No one will ever say I didn't feed my kiddies!

It seemed to Grace that when Anne, Philip, Noel, Sarah sat down to eat they were not eating directly for survival, prestige, love, peace; nor were they alone; nor were they eating in their kitchen at Holly Road, Winchley. Grace had a strange feeling that their meal had been set thousands of years ago: they shared it with all sorts and conditions of people, sitting in a vast hall at a banqueting table extending to a part of the hall where darkness swirled, changing the host from a human being to an invisible presence. Grace could sense the unknown host in the room. She looked at Philip and knew, by the seriousness in his eyes, that the host was important to him; while Anne's face showed a sensuous pleasure in being alive, in sharing a meal at once with so many unknown guests and so few known, intimately loved.

They believe in God, Grace thought, as she observed them. Yet there were no mystical pretensions about their eating. They ate, they talked, they laughed. The children burped and were persuaded to say *Pardon*.

Out of her dream Grace heard Philip talking of New Zealand writers. He was speaking to her.

—Yes? she said, questioning.

—I mean the pre-War ones who are still writing.

Grace recited a list of names.

—I've met some of them, she said, proud to announce that she had some small connection with human beings. Lightly she began to gossip about this and that writer, then stopped suddenly in dismay,

—Oh, I'm gossiping, she exclaimed. —But I'm not saying anything personal. All the same, I'm gossiping.

—Yes, but pleasantly, Philip said.

Grace spoke of guilt-ridden X whose wife worked to keep him.

Philip laughed heartily,

—No danger of that here! *I* bring home the money in this house. He turned from Grace to Anne,

—As soon as these kids are old enough, off you go back to teaching while I retire to the attic and write.

Grace felt alarmed and afraid at his words. She was so fiercely self-centred that she supposed that any strong emotion which affected her must also affect others, and if there were no evidence of this, in her mind she would shake and shake those who had refused to admit her excess emotion, till it seemed that their thoughts dropped out, like poppy-seeds, and they wilted and died . . .

I don't want to return to teaching, she thought, trying to subdue her panic. I can't. There's the scheme to prepare, the work book, the daily attendance, all those little crosses in volumes and volumes, intended in some way to *prove* that a pupil has been absent or present; such an unsophisticated way of recording the movements of human beings; when we know that children are perpetual mental tourists who slip through the most elaborate customs barriers. Morning Talk. Written Expression. Social Studies. Playground duty. The dreaded *morning tea* in the staff room. Conversation with the other probationer, Bill Todd, a vacuous creature for whom I couldn't even feel pity, only resentment that I never had the company of an *interesting* man, never; even when my sister and I paired off with two students it was she who captured the brave intelligent exciting one, while I spent evenings with an inarticulate (no pity, no pity) fool from down south who kept humming a song he had on the brain, *Don't Get Around Much Anymore*.

—What do you say? Go back to teaching?

Grace was stricken with the terrible certainties and uncertainties of speech. Philip had looked at Anne, had spoken to Anne. The ritual of spoken communication is so firmly accepted that few people question it or dare to rearrange it. If you look towards someone, speak to that person, saying You, you, you, then what you say refers to that person; it's all so simple.

Not being a human being and not being practised in the art of verbal communication, Grace was used to experiencing moments of terror when her mind questioned or rearranged the established ritual; when commonplace certainties became, from her point of view, alarming uncertainties. Philip had been speaking to Anne. Yet Grace had been Anne. It was Grace whom Philip addressed now,

—Yes. As soon as these kids are old enough.

Anne smiled calmly, with no hint of having been threatened. She thinks he's talking to her, Grace thought; then, with a sudden unclouding of her head, she returned thankfully to her own identity as Grace, and sat now, listening, listening, fearful of the threat to Anne who smiled again and laughed aloud.

Grace could have wept with relief. So it was all right then, everyone was safe. She stared hard at her plate, in order to pretend, now, that she hadn't heard Philip's words and Anne's smiling reply,

—We'll see about that.

It was a challenge.

Grace prayed to any God who might have been near, Let them not kill each other, please let them not kill each other. He is angry, she is afraid. He will kill her, and be hanged for murder, or strapped in the electric chair in Sing-Sing where they have their own song,

'It's a song they sing at a sing-song in Sing-Sing.
We wish that we were sparrows that we could fly
     away . . .'

Sparrows? Swallows? Cuckoos? The godwits flying 'towards another summer'?

Let all the world be calm, Grace thought. Let Philip not murder Anne. This is my plate, my cheese on toast, this is my coffee in the yellow cup, and – oh my god! – Philip and Anne will kill each other. You see, they are my mother and father.

16

I remember now, Grace said to herself. It was this way:

Sores covered her body and because she could not resist the urge to scratch them they were always bleeding or covered with thin brown scabs; the calves of her legs and her upper arms were marked with great patches of red, and every few minutes as she went about her endless housework she would sit on the coal-bin in the corner by the fire, roll down her stockings, or roll up her sleeves, and begin to scratch; her sores were mapped red like the countries of the British Empire in the *Atlas*. She did not know the name of the disease that afflicted her. She hesitated to mention it to the doctor, that is, Dr Oliver who came to attend to our chickenpox and whooping cough; it was strange that he did not notice her sores. On hot days she wore no stockings and no sleeves. You could see her heavy upper arms that she had once revealed so proudly to us; —Look at my muscle, I could floor any man with that muscle, and we children would go amongst each other displaying our rabbit-giggles of little arms and saying, Look at my muscle, look at my muscle!

The aunt from Dunedin, and my father, and the neighbours who noticed the sores asked,

—Why don't you have them seen to?

But my mother was afraid or proud, or perhaps she thought it might cost too much money, for there was no Social

Security then, and doctors' bills were so impossible that my father used to groan and sigh and then thrust them on the mantelpiece as ornaments and reminders, and soon their transparent windows were sealed with dust.

On the back page of *Truth* there was a weekly feature *Truth's Doctor Tells*. Perhaps my mother wrote to him for advice. I don't know. Or perhaps she sent to a mail order firm. A green ointment with an overpowering smell, like cabbage being cooked in petrol, began to arrive through the post and during the day my mother would sit down to rub the green ointment on her legs. But it was no use. The table in Mum-and-Dad's room was littered with ointment tins, empty except for a smear of melting ointment at the base of the tin. I think that at that time I was as tall as the top of my mother's legs. When I looked at her I could see scabs and running sores. It was like looking at the diseased trunks of two trees – there were such trees in the plantation, their bark rotten and soft with spotted toadstools growing from it and beetles devouring it.

It seemed that for years my mother walked about with her sores, unable to rid herself of them. She no longer ventured outside the gate; soon she did not go very far from the back door. Years afterwards, in her habitual way establishing the period as a crucial time in her life, to be compared with the flood, the time when her arm was 'up for six weeks' and the time when Tommy Lyles was killed, she used to talk of 'When you were little and I didn't go outside the gate for two years.'

I remember that when I lifted my head to look up at her face I would see her crying. If my father had come home and was speaking sharply about the bills and money, I could see that my mother was afraid; or it seemed so; but perhaps it was I who was afraid, but there was my mother with her Godfrey chin and her face like the Archbishop of Canterbury, all in a tremble of tears, and my father saying,

—As soon as these kids are old enough –

—I bring home the money in this house. As soon as these kids are old enough –

Please God let them not kill each other, I said. Let my father not kill my mother because the bills are high and she has sores and the world is full of green ointment, even the green leaves on the pear tree and the plum tree are smelling like green ointment. What will happen when I am old enough? Old enough for what? The cow had a calf and when it was a few weeks old a man came to look at it; he said It's not old enough yet. I said What for? My father said —Don't poke your nose into what doesn't concern you, but the man, unthinking, said, —The freezing works.

Did it snow at the freezing works?

———

—You know what he's doing, don't you love?

That was Philip speaking. Grace was overwhelmed with relief.

Certainly it was Philip speaking. And there was Anne, Sarah, Noel –

Grunt grunt from Noel.

—Yes. Anne smiled. —I guessed as much.

—You're not nice to know, son.

Anne washed and changed the suddenly undesirable and stinking Noel.

—Shall I get the talc, love?

—No thanks. I never use it now.

Philip looked admiringly at Anne, as if by relinquishing powder she had made a kind of sacrifice which he would never have dared to consider. How brave she was! He'd always thought talcum powder was so necessary, as much a part of infancy as nappies. Anne was unhurried, calm, dextrous. Philip's face asked the unspoken question addressed more to the human race than to Noel – Does it have to be like this?

133

He turned apologetically to Grace, almost divining that not being a human being she might seek an explanation.

—Sorry about this. Just one of those things.

—Yes, Anne said looking towards Grace, —we're awfully sorry. They've done nothing but crawl around you since you came and now this has to happen.

—Oh I don't mind, it's *quite* all right.

—But there's a limit, Anne said. —They don't usually hang around visitors in this way.

Grace felt flattered until she realised that there was no peculiar virtue in herself which had made Sarah want to talk to her and Noel crawl over the table to reach her. They behaved thus because they were used to human beings as visitors – people who spoke to them, who perhaps played games with them, who knew what to say, what to do, who did not sit like trees or stones waiting for an invisible power to shift them or speak for them.

—Oh it's *quite* all right, Grace repeated.

And now there was Noel, the little beggar-boy in the night-shirt, ready to be taken up to bed, and Grace felt a fleeting loneliness as she saw him borne away to his infant Styx and Underworld surrounded by the farewell embraces of his family. He had not asked to kiss Grace. Nor did Sarah plead to climb on her knee; she merely said Goodnight, calmly, and followed Anne and Noel upstairs, while Grace, watching them, smiled to herself, remembering that when one is a child and visitors come to stay the first night is for exploration, the second night is for judgment. She remembered the first night's attractive jumble of bags and coats and talkative aunts and uncles, and wanting to stay up to take part in it, to listen, to explore; then on the second night the ordinary calm slightly disillusioned glance about the room at the visitors, seen now in daylight and all day, and the unprotesting journey to bed.

On the third day interest sometimes revived. The pros and

cons had been weighed with awful honesty; the balance was known.

Philip gave a sigh of relief.

—Well that's over.

Grace smiled the understanding smile of the privileged spinster as Philip got up, shook the day from him, went into the sitting room, and sank into the sympathetically embracing armchair by the fire. Grace sat opposite, and comforted by the presence and nearness of books she turned to study the titles. Ah, there was the *Book of New Zealand Verse*!

'O not the self-important celebration
Or most painstaking history, can release
The current of a discoverer's elation
⠀⠀⠀And silence the voices saying,
"Here is the world's end where wonders cease."

Only by a more faithful memory, laying
On him the half-light of a diffident glory,
The Sailor lives, and stands beside us, paying
⠀⠀⠀Out into our time's wave
The stain of blood that writes an island story.'

That, Grace said to herself, a migratory bird instantly in her New Zealand world, was written to commemorate the sailor-explorer Abel Tasman. Perhaps the sailor who helped most to put a stain of blood into our island story was, after all, not Abel Janszoon Tasman, sixteen forty-two sailing the ocean blue, but the American Marine who came during the War to Wellington; that was a time of lust and blood and history when the hearts of all the women came from the wool-sheds and the rabbiters' huts to adventure on the streets of Wellington. I was a school-girl at the time, but I remember we had our fifth-form jokes about the American Marines; and after the War, when they returned to that illusory place 'their own country' (as illusory as a piece of writing which claims to express 'in my own words' – whose words?), the stain of blood showed in all the rivers from the Waikato and Wanganui down to the Clutha; even the mudfilled Mataura had its share of blood mixed with the snow. Now *there* was an effortless Tasman for you, commemorated by no named day or sea!

Philip's eyes were closed. He was recovering from the day; languishing, convalescent.

—Change chairs, so that you can study the books on *this* side of the room. And tomorrow night you can sit in that corner, studying the books there.

He laughed. They exchanged their seats just as Anne entered with a housewifely glance that yet contained the sinister northern exultation of the Macbeth family 'I've done the deed!'

—I've put the children to bed.

—Good.

('A sorry sight. A foolish thought to say a sorry sight . . .')

—Grace and I have changed places so that she can see the books on this side of the room; tomorrow night she's going to sit in that corner.

Philip seemed amused by his plan. Anne, sitting facing the fire, found her place in *Ulysses* and began to read. Philip opened his book on *New Zealand External Affairs*. Grace, unable to select one item from the sudden luxury of reading, studied the titles on the shelves: Architecture; Church Architecture. New Zealand Novels.

—The more I read about him, the more I believe that Peter Fraser was New Zealand's outstanding Prime Minister.

Both Grace and Anne looked up swiftly, defensively. Grace saw in her mind the pathetic cross-eyed bespectacled Prime Minister of whom she knew little and had not cared to know or if she knew she had forgotten. She remembered the attitude towards him which she had absorbed unthinking, sponge-like, from the free-floating stain of public opinion. For the first time she tried to understand her dislike of him; she was appalled to realise that in a 'young' country of 'young' people, sun, beaches, sport, physical health as the ideal perfection, the fact that their Prime Minister had been cross-eyed, had worn spectacles, had seemed unforgivable! He had been regarded as a 'bad' Prime Minister because he wore spectacles.

Grace could have wept with shame. As the poet had commanded, she laid 'a more faithful memory' upon the scene of her country, omitting for once the spellbinding outward landscape, the tourist glaciers, mountains, rivers, plains, bush, so often referred to as if they had been planned glories of a human workshop; concentrating on the personal scenery, the truly human constructions of habit, opinion, prejudice. She watched the smooth golden people with their clear sight, perfect limbs, brains bouncing with sanity and conformity; it seemed they were Life-Guard angels marching from tiny Waipapa beach in the south ('Like to the tide moaning in grief by the shore . . .') to the Northland coast burning with pohutukawas; while the massed bands played – the brass band with the *Invercargill March, Colonel Bogey*; the pipe band with the *Cock o' the North, Speed Bonny Boat*; and the sun shone, the day surged with light, while offshore the tidal wave, restrained for the moment or day or year, bided its drowning time, played its blue patience of wave overlapping numbered wave. Grace observed, with terror, the fanatical innocence of the march, the acceptance of it, the reverence towards it – why, there was her mother, ordinarily a gentle peaceful woman, proclaiming in her confusion of Civil War, God, Country,

'Mine eyes have seen the glory of the coming of the Lord.

137

He is trampling out the vintage where the grapes of
wrath are stored.'

Vintage?

The Life-Guards were trampling sand. Why their sudden
movements of irritation, the spasmodic threshing of their arms
in the air? The sandflies. Of course, they were killing the
sandflies, those tiny black insects which pursued biting, sting-
ing, raising red lumps on the skin; unsightly lumps on the
bronzed beautiful skin.

Grace was so surely on the beach at that moment that
when a drowsy, lazily-observing sunbathing couple turned to
her and said,

—Isn't it wonderful, a great little country, sun, beach,
everyone so healthy?

Grace agreed,

—It's wonderful, the best place in the world to bring up
children; sun, opportunity, health, happiness.

—And soon they'll be getting that stuff to kill off all the
sandflies. Then, it will be even better. It stands to reason that
the sandflies are a nuisance.

—Yes, it stands to reason.

What do you expect, then, when the mad, the crippled, the
unconforming, try to get a place on the beach?

And when a Prime Minister appears, with cross-eyes, spectacles, can't you be expected to dislike him, as you dislike a
sandfly which spoils the parade by making an unsightly red
lump on your perfect skin?

———

—I didn't know much about Peter Fraser, Anne said to
Philip.

—I didn't either, Grace said. —I always think of Mickey
Savage as the great New Zealand Prime Minister.

138

She remembered the huge photograph of Mickey Savage which had covered one wall of their kitchen at home; his gentle face smiling, unscribbled upon, because even as children they had revered him – they could never forget the moments of pure happiness when the notice came from the Health Department that medical and hospital attention were to be free, *free*, and their father had collected all the unpaid hospital and doctors' bills, brushed the dust from their windows, opened them, smoothed them, read them aloud, shuffled them into a pile, and with a shout of joy, pokered the ring from the stove and thrust them into the fire. Grace remembered that their mother's excitement had been tempered with a slight fear that the chimney might be set alight while the hospital bills burned.

—They charge five shillings for a chimney fire!

—Yes, Grace said, unconsciously quoting from her parents,
—Mickey Savage was the one!

(He's the one, her mother would say. —After old Forbes-and-Coates and the Coalition, he's the one! Grace never had a clear understanding of whether Forbes-and-Coates were one or two people or if they were people at all; her image of them was a childish one of coats, black, going green with age, tattered with moth-holes, hanging in a wardrobe; while the word 'Coalition' which she had seen printed made a sound like the shovelling of 'slack', and like slack it seemed something undesirable – the woman next door used to stand in her backyard and call to her son, —Bill, get on more coal, give me no slack!)

—He was the one, Grace murmured.

—Oh yes, Anne agreed.

Grace and Anne exchanged smiles, aware of their sudden bond of sympathy, their New Zealand background and experience overwhelming them with traditional attitudes and statements, their lips set firmly – they would show any

Pommie who tried to tell them what they didn't know about their own country!

The moment was gone in a flash but both Grace and Anne had realised it, their bristling in defence against 'foreigners' (especially 'Pommies'). Grace quoted to herself,

> 'There through her aquid glass
> Circumambient Regina, turning slowly from the pane,
> Is seen imperiously to mouth "Albert, my dear,
> How do we pronounce *Waitangi?*"'

Foreigners were dangerous, especially in a 'young' country. Queers too, outsiders, intellectuals, any doubtful group who might spoil the pleasure of the golden Life-Guards parading the golden beach.

—Certainly, Philip admitted. —Savage introduced Social Security. But it was Peter Fraser who moulded the San Francisco Conference. Almost in opposition to his country it was he who gave New Zealand a voice in World Affairs, who made her look beyond herself for a change; he helped New Zealand in a stage of growing-up.

Oh it's so hard, Grace thought, to care for what one man contributes, invisibly, to the peace of the world, when there's a vivid memory of another who brought peace, for a time at least, into our home set, strangely, in the street of innocence and experience – Fifty-six Eden Street Oamaru South Island New Zealand Southern Hemisphere the World. The world comes so far at the end of the statement; it is so easy to forget it. If I put my list of places to the test by holding them (as they say of the guinea pig) 'upside down by the tail' – Fifty-six Eden Street, Oamaru, South Island, New Zealand, Southern Hemisphere, the World, – it is the world, like the guinea pig's eyes, that would drop out; only places, like guinea pigs, have no tail; they are one; and nothing drops out, ever.

It is so hard to judge. Peter Fraser, Mickey Savage. South, north, the world.

Grace felt suddenly depressed, annoyed by her muddled insular thinking, tired of the 'World' and its problems, lacking the energy to spread her emotional net so wide and the power to pull it home unaided to her heart. She felt lonely; she would sit on a tiny island beach in the sun, or perhaps, after all, she would join the Life-Guards in their march; the massed bands would cheer her, yes, yes, it would be fun to march to the band, and not nearly so uncomfortable now that they had arranged to kill all the sandflies. Sandflies were a nuisance. It stood to reason.

—It stands to reason, her father shouted. What a wonderful phrase that was, what quelling power was contained in it!

—Excuse me . . . I . . . I'll go upstairs for a time – to switch the fire on . . .

—Of course, of course.

Grace escaped upstairs. For a while she huddled over the gas fire, then drawn to the bookshelf and the few books which Anne's father had chosen to bring from New Zealand, she found the *History of the Rifle Brigade*, sat down by the fire and began to read the chapter headed *War in the Trenches*, and while she read she could hear her father singing defiantly, trembling with fear, with disbelief that what was so, was so.

> 'I want to go home,
> I want to go home,
> I don't want to go to the trenches no more
> where the bullets and shrapnel are flying galore.
> Take me over the sea
> where the Allemand won't get at me,
> Oh my,
> I don't want to die,
> I want to go home.'

17

In the clear white-painted cold room which the gas fire could not even begin to warm, Grace read and thought about the First World War, reliving the squalor and terror of it, for though she had not been born until six or seven years after the end of the War, by the convenience of Hollywood, and by the quiet more obscure imaginings gained from her father's talk of war, and the songs he sang about it, she had believed, as a child, that she lived during it, that she had, in fact, 'been to the War', fought in the trenches, suffered wounds by gas and shrapnel.

Nearly every Saturday afternoon at the Majestic Theatre, with her acid drops and aniseed balls in the crisp rustling bag, mixed fairly by the obliging Mrs Widdall so that neither acid drops nor aniseed balls would be left in a monotonous clump at the end of the bag, Grace went to the War, sometimes on the German 'side', sometimes on the side of the 'Allies'. She could not think, without a stifling experience of horror, of the afternoon when she had been trapped under the sea in a submarine shelled by a torpedo. She and her sisters and brother had watched the serial, *The Ghost City*, and although they realised that cowboys and rustlers were 'pretend', they had been given their following week's quota of nightmare by the ending of the day's episode where the 'goodie' entered the shed of a deserted quarry while unknown to him the 'baddie' set in operation the huge stone-crusher; slowly, slowly it began to descend on him; he could not escape; the episode ended in a crash of music and hooves and it was time for ice-creams.

Then the lights were put out and Grace and her sisters and brother found themselves under the sea in a submarine, in danger of being suffocated or drowned. Every time they tried to forget their danger the picture reminded them by showing the water gradually rising and the other members of the crew gasping for breath, collapsing, going mad with panic. Suffocation. It was a terrifying word. Grace could never forget the yellow gleam of the underwater light, not the colour of sunlight, for it lay so far from the sun that light had never touched it; a yellow sulphurous glow which reminded her of the last day of Pompeii — another catastrophe experienced and real in the confusion of remembering, knowing, dreaming, which seem to funnel all events read, heard or known, drop by drop into the containing pool of a child's memory.

When the picture finished, and Grace and her sisters and brother trooped out, blinking, into the harsh sandpaper daylight so different from the soft secret gleam beneath the sea, they knew, or rather Grace knew, and she took it for granted that the others knew also, that the world had changed; it would never ever be the same. Grace looked at the people spilling out of the *Exits*; she almost felt that she could not breathe for thinking about their doom of suffocation and death. Although she had never noticed it before, she knew as she watched them that they were finding difficulty in breathing on and on and on, yet they were not under the sea, they were up here in the world, on the earth, with the sun shining, the daylight twinkling and birds singing and the leaves on the trees turning yellow and brown and gold and in the garden of the big two-storeyed red brick house where Miss Peters lived, the three sycamore trees leaning into the street were also turning gold.

—The sycamores are ripe, Grace thought, springing and skipping suddenly. —The sycamores are ripe.

That meant they were ready for windmills. On the way home from the pictures they made windmills from the sycamores, running along the street with them, but every third or fourth skip they remembered and knew that making windmills and running along in the wind couldn't change the fact that people, even those walking about with plenty of air in the sky and all the world, were growing more and more frightened of not being able to breathe, of suffocating in a secret place withdrawn from the sun where the light, though softened by water, gleamed yellow as the volcanic fire on that last day of Pompeii . . . Pompeii . . . Grace remembered that her mother had been there too, how she had called their attention to the rumbling of the volcano, and then stood quite still, holding aside the curtain of the kitchen window and saying in a voice shrill with disaster, —Pompeii. Pompeii.

But the War, the First War . . .

———

Outside the Red Cross shanty hospital the wounded were arranged in neat rows, like schoolboys in dormitories under the sky, but they were nowhere, really, except on page fifty-three of the *History of the Rifle Brigade*. Grace could have turned the pages quickly to be rid of them. Why should she worry about soldiers wounded in the First World War when there were so many soldiers and so many wars?

The General was making his inspection. See, his bones picked clean resembled the bones of all other men, but take pity on him, restore his carpet of flesh, wrap him in it, erase all wounds; he is the General.

He addressed the men,

—If you are captured by the enemy what is the procedure?

144

A chorus from the wounded, their voices quavering like those of old old men,

—Name rank number, name rank number.

Grace was about to turn from page fifty-three to page fifty-five when one of the wounded, lying with his companions, so neatly arranged and lion-stamped, tucked into their narrow grey stretchers like supplies of standard eggs fitted into cardboard containers, wriggled himself up on his elbow, jerked his head high, dared to draw attention to himself.

Grace was powerless to turn the page until she had heard him speak. He said, in a cringing tone from which all pride had gone, strained, as it were, through the final perforations of reality,

—Notice me! Notice me! Tell the General to notice me, how badly wounded I am. Promise!

— I promise, Grace said.

As she was closing the book she heard him singing in a voice of hysterical gaiety,

'I want to go home,
I want to go home,
I don't want to go to the trenches no more
where the bullets and shrapnel are flying galore.
Take me over the sea
where the Allemand won't get at me,
Oh my,
I don't want to die,
I want to go home.'

Replacing the book on the shelf, Grace switched off the gas fire and went downstairs to the sitting room. Philip and Anne looked up as she entered. Philip's eyes showed a mixture of sympathy and alarm, and Anne said hurriedly,

—Would you like a cup of coffee?

145

—Yes please, Grace said, and then explaining her absence, —I got caught with your father's book, *The Story of the Rifle Brigade*. I've been reading for about an hour.

—You had the fire on, I hope?

Grace wanted to say, Why, no!, to make Philip and Anne believe that she was either too timid or too absorbed to turn on the fire, but she was a passionate seeker for Truth, whatever it may be, even in little things, and she would have the world without and the world within stripped of all deceit, in the way that the birds, flying down to seize the flakes of gold that covered the Happy Prince, had stolen his clothes, then his limbs, his jewelled eyes, his ears, his flesh until only his heart remained . . . one had to begin, carefully removing deceit layer by layer . . . therefore Grace answered,

—Yes, I turned on the fire.

She had not been too timid, too absorbed; it was an act, because she felt she did not measure up to their expectation of her; they had expected a witty, wise, intelligent guest; instead they had this Grace-Cleave, as hyphenated as her name when it was spoken (intuitively) by little Sarah.

Yet she was indeed afraid, chiefly of thresholds and the human beings who might cross them; continually warned, she gave forth an offensive cloud of emotion and dream – timidity, absorption.

—Yes, she repeated boldly, —I turned on the fire.

She saw that, secretly, Philip and Anne wished she had not been so bold. They had been concerned for her going to her room and staying there an hour or more without a word of explanation. They had wanted to be able to say, anxiously,

—Oh you should have turned on the fire to warm the room. You must use it at any time, Grace.

She observed their disappointment, their cautious pruning from their words of the anxiety that was not, after all, necessary.

—I'm glad you were warm enough, they said together.

—Was your father in the Rifle Brigade? Grace asked Anne.

—Yes. Look, I'll make coffee.

When Anne returned and they had drunk their coffee, Grace pulled a book, *Modern Architecture*, from the shelves, and sprang with quick courage to her feet.

—I think I'll retire. Goodnight.

Goodnight, Philip and Anne said together, Philip adding, again as if there were some doubt about her appearing in the morning,

—See you in the morning.

—Yes, she said formally.

Dear Sir, with regard to your statement on the matter of Sunday morning, this is to confirm . . .

She would never learn; communication with people was more than a business letter; why could she not make it so? There were tears of rage in her eyes, rage at herself and the World, as tripping over insts, ults, res, and heretofores, she went upstairs to bed.

As on her first night at Winchley, her pillow was wet with tears before sleep came.

18

She woke during the night. Her mouth throbbed. Is it words or toothache?

Toothache starts and is stopped with violence masked or revealed.

—Smell the pretty towel, the dentist said to Grace, and obligingly she lifted her head, sniffing at the pretty pink towel; then choking with the deceit of it she struggled, bit, kicked, but it was no use, the dentist won, by telling lies he had won, and soon Grace was asleep, and when she woke the tooth was gone, there was a ragged hollow in her mouth and a taste of blood, the special taste that you know is blood and that makes you say, while you see it in your mind red, flowing down wide wide stone steps into the sun and the market-place, —It's blood, I can taste blood. When the tooth was gone there was no more crying in the night and smacked bottom at night because she cried, there was only the new discomfort – Grace was getting too big for her cot, her legs went against the bars when she tried to stretch them. She was four now, and her favourite music was the bagpipe music played by their father as he walked up and down the passage in the evening.

—Play me to sleep, Dad. Bagpipe me to sleep. Quick, I'll get into my cot and you bagpipe me to sleep!

And their father played them to sleep, mostly with the full

bagpipes, squashing the bag rhythmically with his arm as he walked so that it made a faint wheezing sound, like Grandad under the music; other times without the bag and the pipes spread like fingers and the hanging tartan fringes, the kilt, the sporran, only in ordinary home-from-work clothes, standing still, playing the chanter; explaining, with a resignation that seemed frightening, there was not even the stir of a struggle in it, that one day he'd never be able to play the bagpipes again, he'd only be able to manage the chanter, and then, gradually, not even the chanter.

—Some day, he said, I won't have the wind.

How strange to pass from the brilliant paraphernalia of bagpipe and kilt to the shorn, drab chanter which never captured the full gurgle and skirl and wail of Highland glens and hills; and from the chanter to go, very quietly, almost not caring, to nothing; a valve of life closing, sealed for ever.

And it happened as Grace's father had predicted. A time came when he no longer played the bagpipes and when the chanter lay disused in its box in the sideboard; the kilt went astray on one of the many 'shifts', and Grace and her sisters and brother played beards and Santa Claus with the sporran.

—Bagpipe me to sleep!

He sang to them, too.

'Come for a trip in my airship,' he sang.

And,

'Underneath the gas light's glitter
stands a little orphan-girl . . .'

Who?
Not me.
Not me.
'I belong to Glasgow, dear old Glasgow town.'

'He wheels his wheel-barrow,
through streets broad and narrow,
crying cockles and mussels alive-alive-oh . . .'

And the song which made the little sister, Dots, who was nearly three, run to hide under the table, sobbing and sobbing, while the others watched in pity for her; their hearts turned to ice when they heard the song but only little Dots was moved to tears. Supposing . . .

'Don't go down in the mine, Dad,
dreams very often come true.
Daddy you know it would break my heart
if anything happened to you . . .'

Oh why did their father torture them by singing it? He wasn't a miner, he was a first-class engine-driver, *locomotive engineer* he described himself in his time-sheets and when there were papers from school to be filled in, saying what their father *did*; yet perhaps he was, after all, a miner? Everything was so *possible*. Possibility was not a bag or box that could be closed and sealed, it was a vast open chute which received everything, everything; one could not choose or direct or destroy the powerful flow of possibility.

—There's no such word as *can't*! their father would say to them sternly, and although they tried to understand, to reason the matter, they could only grasp that he spoke the truth; they learned, also, that there was no such word as *isn't* or *wasn't*. Apparently, everything *was*. Dragons? Even dragons. And God.

So their father was a first-class engine-driver, yet at the same time he was a miner going down the mine to his death because his little daughter, Dots, with the fair hair, had dreamed it all, had dreamed that he died.

When their mother sang to them at night she seldom sang

150

unhappy songs; sometimes they were puzzled and confused by words which were meant to make them laugh, but they did not laugh, they frowned, saying Why? Why? How can it be? How can Grandma's uncle die with the pip? Which pip?

'Grandma's uncle died with the pip,
you tell Dinah that.'

Their mother disapproved of sad songs. She reproached their father for making the children cry with fear when he sang *The Wearing of the Green*.

'They're hanging men and women at the wearing of
the green.'

Hanging men and women! Their mother said, —Never mind, kiddies, don't think about it, it's only a song, think of fairies and angels and God in Heaven . . . But angels were beings so difficult to think about, their life seemed silly, they weren't men or women, they didn't eat, they didn't go to the lavatory or speak, they merely flew around in the clouds or walked on earth in disguise . . . now that was more interesting . . . one never knew . . .
    —Why did they hang men and women at the wearing of the Green?
    —Don't sing it, Curly.
    —Sing *Ragtime Cowboy Joe*, Dad!
    This was an action song; their father had to get up to dance to it. He was Ragtime Cowboy Joe.

'Way out in Arizona where the bad men are,
the only thing to guide you is an evening star,
roughest toughest man by far
is Ragtime Cowboy Joe.

When he starts a-shooting on the dance-hall floor
no one but a lunatic would start a war,
wise men know his forty-four
makes men dance for fear,

he always sings
raggy music to the cattle as he swings
back and forward in the saddle on the *hoss*
he's a high falutin' scootin' shootin'
son-of-a-gun from Arizona,

Ragtime Cowboy Joe . . .'

—Now *Dan Murphy*, Dad.

That was their special song, because a Mr Murphy lived over the road, and his doorstep was a stone doorstep with green moss growing on it.

—'Twas long years ago . . . their father would begin, and, put into the right mood of sadness they would wait for him to sing the special part about *them*. He would look at them proudly; how noble they felt!

'Contented although we were poor . . .
and the songs that we sung
in the days we were young
on the stone outside Dan Murphy's door.
Those friends and companions of childhood . . .'

This last line was always sung in a warble which cracked at the end as it became louder; it was a pathetic loudness and boldness which stayed in Grace's memory; she could still hear her father singing it, for it held one of those unidentifiable qualifications which so often admit to permanent memory the most common-place unexpected events, words, snatches of sentence and song.

In spite of her objections to 'sad' songs their mother had a full verse repertoire of wars, floods, tidal waves. There was a dog which pined and died at his master's grave – the refrain at the end of each verse went

'The dog at his master's grave . . .'

There were little crippled boys, orphaned girls; but their mother's favourites were poems dealing with universal rather than personal disasters. Floods haunted her. Grace knew, by the way her mother spoke, that she had been there, in the Ark, with Noah and the animals; that she had been on the coast of Lincolnshire during the High Tide.

'The old mayor climbed the belfry tower.'

(Grace saw the old mayor in his wide black hat, in his skinny stockinged legs with red garters, spidering his way up the narrow stairs.)

Then the cows coming home (like Betty, Beauty, Pansy) –

'Cusha Cusha Cusha calling
ere the early dews were falling,
Come up Whitefoot, Come up Lightfoot,
Jetty to the milking-shed.'

But Grace knew that although cows waited to be milked and Beauty and Pansy were docile they did not always obey the call to the milking-shed – the cow-byre; there was one cow, named Scrapers because she fastidiously scraped her hooves before entering the byre, who had to be led with a rope around her horns and whose progress, instead of being through a gentle meadow of daisies and primroses, was down a steep path beside limestone cliffs with a creek in the gully over which she had to be persuaded to jump. Yet Whitefoot, Lightfoot, Jetty, Beauty, Pansy, Scrapers, lived within sound of the sea and (Grace always supposed) in the threat of a tidal wave – it was Grace's mother who made it so – did she not look fearfully from the window towards the Breakwater, Cape Wanbrow, the Pacific Ocean roaring so near, while she told them of Mary, of the Sands of Dee,

> 'Oh Mary go and call the cattle home
> and call the cattle home
> across the Sands of Dee,
> the western wind was wild and dank with foam,
> and all alone went she.'

In the end, Mary was drowned in the tide, and in spite of the fact that Grace's life was so different from Mary's (It was —Grace! Grace! Go and get the cows, it's time they were milked), there was always the sea so near, threatening, swallowing the land.

—When I was a kid there was a football ground where the sea is now, their father would say in a tone of wonder. The loss of a football field was serious. Sometimes professors toured the country lecturing on *Erosion, The Sea's Threat to the Land*, showing lantern slides of ordinary land scarred, undermined, swallowed by waves, but none of their lectures could rouse the imagination as completely as the impressive fact that a *football field* had disappeared . . .

Often Grace used to look from the window, waiting for the tidal wave, or stamp on the wooden floor of the kitchen, to read the secrets of the earth beneath, to be warned of the earthquake which would rise from what their mother called the 'bowels' of the earth. Often the house began to shake, chimneys toppled in the streets, and with the dread memory of the San Francisco and Napier earthquakes vivid in her mind, their mother gave instructions which always confused Grace who could never decide whether she had been told to 'run out into the streets, clear of the houses' or 'stay in the house; the last thing to do is to go out into the streets', with the result that whenever the earth began to shake (their town was on a fault line) by the time Grace had stopped to *reason* a course of action, the earthquake was over, their mother was sighing and saying, —Thank God it's not going to be like Napier, and, if he were at home, their father, pretending as usual, would comment mildly, —I can't see what all the fuss is about.

The fuss, of course, was Death. Grace knew that. She realised, too, that death did not often come from the earth or the sea, that it was there, at home, living with them in the way their grandma lived with them and no one asked her to go away. There was more reason, then, to make a 'fuss' when death had the impertinence to ally itself with earth and sea and (in thunder and lightning) with the sky.

No, death lived with them, like their grandma. Oh Grandma! She sang too, why were the grownups singing and singing, their mother singing and reciting when she swept and cleaned, cooked and fed, their father singing when he came home from work and had a bath (though he was quiet when he shaved; he was terrifying; he could not bear to be peeped at —Why can't we watch you shaving, Dad? —By the Lord Harry clear out I say!), and their grandma sang, sitting in her wheelchair in the sun, and it was the songs of her grandma that made Grace want to cry. She was aware, in a strange way, that grandma was 'somebody else'; she was not mother nor father, their home was not her real home, and often when she sat outside in the sun she seemed not to have any place to belong, as if she had wheeled her chair in from the street, to a strange place, and soon would wheel it away again, to another strange place. She was big, with three or four chins, dark eyes, black frizzy hair, and she wore a long black dress. People said she came from 'Glasgow way', six months in the ship when she was only eighteen, but Grace knew that she had been a slave in Virginia, America, for in her songs she sang of homesickness for 'Virginie'. Her longing for 'Virginie' seemed to

Grace the same kind of longing she felt for the hide-out in the silver birch trees, for the place the wind sang of when it moaned in the telegraph wires along the hot dusty road.

> 'Carry me back to ole Virginie,
> there's where the cotton an' the corn an' taters grow,
> there's where the birds warble sweet in the springtime,
> there's where my ole darkie's heart am long to go . . .'

Or, in a cheerful mood, she sang, jerking her elbows to the rhythm,

> 'Down in the cane-brake that's where I'm goin'
> down where the mocking-bird is singin' mighty low.
> Come along, come, the boat lies low,
> we'll sail high an' dry on the O-hi-O,
> Come along, come, the boat lies low,
> we'll sail high 'n' dry on the O-hi-O . . .'

Yes, Grace thought, I'll come. Quick, quick.

———

The house was silent. Philip and Anne were asleep, the children were asleep. No singing. Two nights and one day at Winchley and no singing except for Noel's morning song of combined praise, renewal, reminder of being: in an infant voice that yet had no intelligible words. Silence was a city discipline which Grace found hard to bear; one did not burst into loud tuneless singing if one lived in a flat with people below, above, through this wall and that wall. One had to be 'civilised'. One bought gramophone records of other people's music, of artists who could sing beyond the simple statement *I want to go home, Oh My I don't want to die, I want to go home.*
    In my country, Grace thought – yes, I'm saying it, *in my*

country – the sky and cloud used to be above, the grass and the dead below, and through this wall and that wall sheep and cattle and the wind from the Southern Alps. But I'm in a different world now, I'm completing the act of finding by losing – 'finds keeps loses weeps'.

I'm in Noel's grandfather's room. Sarah's grandfather. His bagpipe music is on the bookshelf. I notice there are records of bagpipe music on one of the shelves. *Cock o' the North, The Wee MacGregor, The Massed Pipe Bands of the Highlands* . . .

Grace felt tears in her eyes. Finds keeps loses weeps. 'Finding is the first act, the second, loss.' Her eyes felt like pits of sand. They think I'm returning to London on Monday, she thought, but I can't stay, I can't stay, I'll leave tomorrow, I'll forget about *in my country, in my country*, I'll sit in the London flat making my civilised voyage of discovery, and hope that people above, below, next door do not surround me so much that I no longer set out like Abel Tasman 'in a new direction' to 'enlarge the world' or follow my destined course as a migratory bird.

Let me not become a ship-and-sailor strangled in a bottle, a glass bird upon a mantelpiece!

19

I remember, she said. I remember it was this way:

School starts and goes on and on. I think I am learning to read. I have a book with big black print and a soft green cover with pale green threads running through it. The first story is of *Little Red Riding Hood* who set out one day to take some sweetmeats (what are sweetmeats?) to her grandmother, not knowing that a wolf had been into the house in the wood – see his open jaws, his teeth, his red tongue like flannel? – and had gobbled up grandma, had dressed himself in her clothes, and was waiting to gobble up Red Riding Hood. It seems that people in stories may or may not hear you speak to them, yet nothing you say can change the story as it is written. How can I warn Red Riding Hood? The words of the story are spread over the whole page, there is no room for me to write a warning, and if I put *Watch Out Red Riding Hood* at the bottom of the page or in the margin, I'm sure Red Riding Hood will not heed it, and, strange to say, I'm glad, for by the time she has reached the little house deep in the wood (why don't they say the 'bush'? And why are there always robins and nightingales and no fantails?) I look forward with enjoyment to the moment when she opens the door, goes to the bedroom, gets into bed with grandmother, and is gobbled up by the wolf – how disappointing that a huntsman should be passing just as the wolf is about to eat Red Riding Hood! If a wolf dressed as my grandma I should know at once – or should I? It's easy to make a mistake about people . . . people's faces change . . . sometimes people look like wolves . . . how silly.

There's no need to be afraid, oh no. To get home from school I merely go down one street, turn into another, go down it, cross the railway line, and I'm home. How could a wolf possibly get there first: if I hurry?

I like reading. Once the words are on the page they never change; when you open the book the print never falls out.

She's learning to read; she's in the primers; she's going to be a school-teacher when she grows up; she goes to Wyndham District High School.

—What are you learning at school?

—I'm learning a song,

'If the doctor, spectacles on nose,
feels your pulse and says, Well I suppose
a dose of castor-oil will be the best,
How'd you like to be a baby girl?'

—Who's your teacher?

—Miss Botting but we call her Miss Bottom.

—Let me see your reading book. You're getting to be a big girl, reading this, aren't you?

—Yes, I'm a big girl. Yes yes yes yes.

All the same I'm wondering why so many stories are of boys and girls who set out with a message or to make a journey and never deliver the message or reach the end of the journey because they are seized by wolves and foxes. I never knew there were so many wolves and foxes in the world. My mother sings a song called, *New Zealand the land of the fern* and when she has finished singing she likes to tell us that we have no

159

snakes or wolves or foxes or wild animals in our country. My father looks stern, 'All things are possible.' 'Make sure you don't speak too soon.'

Perhaps when I go to school tomorrow I shan't be as lucky as the boy who was swallowed by the fox and rescued alive from the fox's belly. It is dark and mysterious inside a belly, with slimy machinery moving around you and moss growing red like blood upon the walls, and bare knuckles separated from hands and fingers and floating in a green and yellow swamp; *knuckles*; look at my *knuckles*, look at my *shins*; over the railway line, past the clump of wild sweet peas, inside the gorse hedge is a perfect hidey-hole for any fox who wanted to swallow children on their way to school.

We have a new baby.

My grandma is dead.

If you knew you had *knuckles* and *shins* wouldn't you cry and cry?

———

My grandma's death was the smoothest death I ever knew, like a slow dance, and my mother ironed my father's best suit and his black tie, and grandma lay in her bedroom, to be looked at, but nobody asked me to look at her. The aunt from Dunedin and the aunt from Wellington had wet faces and lips and they turned slowly round and round, there, by the door from the passage to the kitchen, and said to Isy, my eldest sister,

—Would you like to see Grandma?

Slowly, carefully, they walked along the passage, and Isy saw Grandma, and was given a life-time of teasing-power, —I saw Grandma when she was dead and you didn't see her. I saw Grandma when she was dead.

—What did she look like?

—She looked asleep.

160

It was no use my saying I didn't believe her because I *had* to believe her, because only she *knew*, and I couldn't put grandma into a book and try to get her to answer if I wrote in the margin *Grandma do you look asleep now you are dead?*

—You *can't* look asleep if you have *stopped.*

—Grandma did. All dead people do.

—But you *must* look different when you've stopped. You can't breathe. You've finished breathing. Hold your breath.

—All right. You hold yours. Go on, I'm holding mine, I'm holding mine –

—I'm holding mine. Oh Oh I'm suffocating, Mum Isy's made me *suffocate!*

Suffocate. Suffocate.

—And here comes Dad to strap us or bagpipe us, one or the other.

———

At school there are people who are here one minute and gone the next and there are people who stay for ever. Billy Delamare stays, but only because he messed his pants at school. Margaret Wilmot stays because her father is the headmaster and on her birthday she wore her best dress and walked up on the platform in the classroom and Miss Botting said,

—Margaret, here is a present from your father for your birthday. Happy birthday, Margaret!

Miss Botting asked us to shout, Happy Birthday Margaret.

Oh to be the headmaster's daughter and wear a best dress and be shouted at, Happy Birthday!

—See what the present is, Margaret, Miss Botting urged.
—Open the envelope and look inside.

Margaret Wilmot needed no second telling. She was hesitating only for effect. She opened the envelope, took out the present and showed it to Miss Botting who let out a cry of delight and turned to the class, waving in her hand Margaret Wilmot's birthday present.

—Now isn't she a lucky girl, children? Margaret's father has given her a pound note for her birthday. A *pound note*, she emphasised, trying to convey the fact that this was an occasion, and suitably pleased when there was a hush-sh-sh, then silence, then gasps of O-oh-Oh, as everyone realised that a pound note was the most wonderful present anyone could have. Why then, when we played the game of presents and I said to my mother,

—What do you want Santa Claus to bring you, did she answer,

—Kind words and a happy home.

Certainly when my mother said that my father usually said, quickly,

—Rot.

But he didn't request a pound note. He wanted the wolf kept from the door.

So he knew then, he knew about the wolves and foxes on the way to school, and the little boy who had been trapped inside the fox's belly!

—Margaret Wilmot's father gave her a pound note for her birthday. She went up on the platform and Miss Botting gave it to her in an envelope and she opened it and waved it at us. A pound note.

—She must be a show-off, my father said.

—Fancy a child so young having a pound note for her birthday! my mother said.

It seemed that they'd never be following the example of Mr Wilmot. *I'd* never be standing on the platform having the teacher wave a pound note at the class. The only time I'd been on the platform was when they found me out as a thief.

The next day when I went to school I looked contemptuously at Margaret Wilmot as if to say (it was easiest to think and say what one's mother and father had thought and said)

—You're a show-off, a skite!

I was promoted to Primer Two. A few weeks later I skipped up to Standard One, Mr Ryan's class.

—Pay attention, Mr Ryan said, and he strapped me. Why did they always talk of *paying* attention?

Then the news came.

—Another shift, Mum. Up north. To Oamaru. Oamaru? Where's that?

—In Otago.

—Up Central?

—No, the Coast.

—They have earthquakes in Oamaru, don't they? I've read of them in the *Wyndham Farmer*. And the sea's eating away the land.

My mother could put such terror into the universe, merely by saying a few words, widening her eyes, putting her hand on her heart, or looking swiftly over her shoulder at an unseen enemy, in this case the earth's 'bowels', the 'sea's hunger'.

—Look up Oamaru in the map then. Dad, where's the *Atlas*?

—Which *Atlas*? First I heard of an *Atlas*. There's a map though in *Pears' Dictionary* but you won't find it there, oh no, just places like Europe, Africa, America. Oamaru's not there!

My father sounded secretive, as if it were he who had hidden Oamaru from those who sat in their office in London, choosing important places for the *Atlas*.

Hurrah, a shift, a shift!

My father played golf on Sundays and we unravelled the golf balls to see what they were made of; and my newest sister was

163

crawling round her box doing mess like cooked cauliflower in her nappies, and I had worms. Worms. I saw them! I looked down after I had finished one day and there were little white things wriggling and crawling in it, and I said, Mum, there are all little white things in it, wriggling!

—Worms! my mother said, in a horrified voice. —Worms!

She frightened me. I made up my mind to keep my mouth shut in future.

—The child's got worms, my mother said to my father.

My father exclaimed, looking fiercely at me,

—Worms?

Guilty, alarmed, I whispered, —Please may I leave the table, and I went outside and sat among the daisies and dandelions in the grass, all by myself, because I had worms.

Noel is singing. It is morning again. Philip and Anne and the children are getting up. I hear them downstairs now. It must be ten o'clock in the morning, Sunday. Why stop at God? Why make Him lid, blanket, roof of human mythology? Because, reaching God, we are wordless, why grow afraid and stop in our journey, why not continue, singing at first, as Noel sings when he awakes, the unintelligible words that one by one will blossom into the new language?

20

Grace prepared her speech.

—By the way, I think I'll go back to London this afternoon. I intended to stay until Monday but I find I'm missing my typewriter, I'd like to be working again . . . you know?

By the way. I'm afraid. You know . . .

Bacon cooking, bathroom taps being turned on, off, cisterns flushing, movements up, down stairs, children's voices pleading (for food); yawns, sleep-filled exclamations; silence.

Certain of the accuracy of her Sunday morning judgment, Grace got up, washed, dressed, waited ten minutes counting the seed potatoes in rows from the right, in rows from the left, then walked slowly downstairs to the warm kitchen; anticipating the scene there – the children, dressed and fed, playing quietly with their books or toys, Philip and Anne sitting at the table, the breakfast ready –

—Good morning. We're just about to begin. You chose the exact moment to come down to breakfast. Not every guest has an instinctive sense of timing . . .

She heard herself answering,

—It's practice. I've learned to live edge to edge with Time, fitting each moment as pinked not ragged seams are fitted; no frayed moments. It's an art, that is, a necessity; don't you think so? Even for those who are not migratory birds like myself. You know I'm a migratory bird? A sooty shearwater, godwit, swallow, common thrush – I heard the thrush singing on a Spanish island in an olive tree with the light lying in patches of snow upon the smooth grey stones.

The restriction of the delights and dangers of overlapping oneself, obscuring each pointed moment, have been replaced by the perfect view one gets, beyond Time, if one tailors one's movements and needs to fit it.

Now they were answering, with admiration at her wisdom,

—Yes. True, true, true.

And she was saying,

—When our thoughts revolve we are so often deceived into supposing that their violent movement is an indication of their vigorous originality, the upheaval of prejudice and fixed ideas, when all the time it is more likely that the machine which contains them is only an elaborate cement-mixer, and when the thinking is finished, those whirling thoughts are smoothed into the unchanged conventional mould and seeing them set solid enough to dance, to build, to travel upon, we would never dream of their first deceit, of the hope once roused by their apparently violent reorganisation . . .

Then Philip, leaning back in his chair, pushing his empty plate aside, was saying, —Let's talk of this. Let's talk. A little less . . . pompously perhaps, but do you know, Grace, do you know . . .

—Yes, yes, Grace was saying eagerly,

—Let's talk. Let's talk of Time, of pinked seams fitting edge to edge, of cement-mixers on building sites, let's go far out where images dangle and float, let's peg them to concepts, make a circus, a Sunday morning circus: the lion, the tiger, the fat man with his laden table in front of him, the barker or placard explaining, Do you know how many pounds of food the fat man needs each day? Enough for a man, his wife, three children to feed upon – and more! And more! See the table sway with the weight of the food, try for yourself, eat a fat man's meal, free admission for those who undertake to eat a fat man's meal . . .

—Isn't this rather . . . extravagant, for Sunday morning, Anne was saying.

—It rains, a gale rises, the big top collapses, fire breaks out, panic, people trample their neighbours to death as faced with the prospect of dying they make the decision, now, swiftly, who matters most. I matter. I. I. I matter. Philip, Anne, Noel, Sarah, listen to me. I matter. I fly alone, apart from the flock, on long journeys through storm and clear skies to another summer. Hear me!

———

When Grace entered the kitchen she found Anne feeding Noel his breakfast while Sarah played with her doll. There was no other food upon the table; nothing was prepared. Philip was nowhere to be seen.

Feeling that retreat was out of the question, Grace sat awkwardly at the table.

—Good morning, Anne said. —Would you like a cup of coffee before breakfast?

—No, no thank you. I'm afraid I'm much too early. I have no sense of time. I thought . . . I don't know . . . It's dark at night here isn't it . . . different from London. By the way, I think I'll return to London this afternoon instead of tomorrow morning. I think I'm homesick for my typewriter. I'd love to stay until tomorrow morning but I *really am* homesick for my typewriter . . . it's been wonderful here, I've enjoyed it so much, thank you for asking me, I . . . I . . . I . . .

—Well if you feel you have to, but you're welcome to stay, but if you feel you have to.

Oh, Grace thought. I should have waited until she and Philip were together. Now I must repeat my excuses to Philip. Oh dear, oh dear.

Philip came in, dressed in his best suit.

—Good morning. Did you sleep well?

As on the previous morning, Grace was embarrassed by his question for his insistent glance seemed to expect a detailed reply, perhaps an account of dreams dreamed. He looked dissatisfied when Grace said merely Good morning; yes thank you. There was silence while he waited, smiling, encouraging, eager to *know*.

Grace said nothing. Anne, releasing Noel at last from his high chair, looked across at Philip.

—Grace is returning to London this afternoon. She's eager to get back to work.

Spoken by others, one's excuses never have the kindly camouflage provided by one's own speech; they emerge sharply outlined, unmistakably recognisable as excuses. Horrified to hear her own words being put about, so uncared for, so unplanned for, with no attempt to disguise or pamper them, Grace seized them, rearranged them, thrust them urgently towards Philip,

—I'm enjoying myself very much here, but I do really think that I'll return to London this afternoon. I feel that I need to work at my typewriter. I do. Really. I'd love to stay. I'd love to stay.

Philip looked disappointed and hurt.

—But there's my study upstairs. You can go there any time, use my typewriter, stay up there as long as you like; you don't have to go back to London. Use my typewriter.

—But it's not the same, it's not the same, Grace said, her voice rising to drown her own guilt.

—It's not the same, she repeated, this time in a shrill bantering tone, trying to sound gay and humorous, but feeling foolish and depressed when Philip's response came, neither lighthearted nor understanding but chilled with brevity and fact and his sense of having failed as a host,

—Well if you must go then . . . I'll look up the trains. But you know you can use my study, and stay as long as you like.

—Of course. I don't want to leave. I want very much to stay. It's just that I'm homesick for my typewriter.

The subject was dismissed. Philip was ready for church.

—I'm away now, he said.

—Daddy, can I come to church with you?

—Not this morning, Sarah. There may be a family service later in the day. You can come then.

Philip went to Anne and gave her a brief kiss while Grace looked at them out of the corner of her eye, noting the absence of outward feeling in their kiss. They had so coded their love that they could express it in one simple common-place gesture, as a painter who has practised his art for years is able without loss of dignity or skill to produce for public inspection a canvas composed of one straight line or painted wholly in one colour. As those who study the painting are at first and perhaps for ever undecided whether it is a simple concentration of nothing or of something, Grace mused on the apparent and real feeling expressed by the kiss, but the galleries of love retained their secret. When Philip and Anne invited her for the weekend they did not promise to give her a catalogue of their still and moving life in flesh and spirit.

———

Grace had her breakfast alone. Then she and Anne drank coffee together. Noel was tucked to sleep in his pram outside, Sarah was nursing a towelled spoon-angel while baby Jesus, out of fashion, lay on the floor.

—Do you like cooking? Do you cook for yourself in London?

—Yes, I like cooking. I don't bother much, on my own.

—I had a friend over from New Zealand, I went to London to see her, and here she was in this Earls Court bedsitting room with a poky gas ring in the corner. She asked me to have a meal. She threw everything into one pot – vegetables, meat, everything, broke an egg into it, and served it as it was, water and all. Water and all!

—Oh yes, Grace said excitedly. —I know. I know. I knew someone with a tiny electric ring in the corner of the room. She used to get up at about three o'clock in the morning to put the kettle on, to have it boiled by breakfast-time at seven o'clock. That's a slight exaggeration . . . of course.

—But the water in all the vegetables! And margarine, not butter, blobbed in it!

—I know, I know!

—And I've another friend over from New Zealand. She comes to stay with us. She burps. It sounds ridiculous but she burps, in quite an uninhibited fashion. It's the strangest sound I've ever heard. She claims not to be able to help it. She does it everywhere, everywhere at any time.

Anne tried to give a demonstration of her friend's peculiar noise.

They laughed together.

—Philip was very brave to take her to Holy Communion in Relham Cathedral.

Grace felt a stab of jealousy.

They were silent for a while.

—You don't mind my staying here in the kitchen? I like being here. It's warm, and it's nice, just talking. I noticed upstairs in your father's room – bagpipe music. Does he play the bagpipes?

—He used to play. He used to walk up and down the passage playing the bagpipes.

—Up and down the passage? But my father did too! He used to play us to sleep at night. But when we shifted to Oamaru he didn't play the bagpipes any more, only the chanter–

170

—Oh yes, the chanter. Dad's got his chanter here with him, but he doesn't play it any more.

—'I haven't the wind' my father used to say. 'I can't play the bagpipes any more, and now not even the chanter' . . . Did your father wear a kilt?

—He had one. He didn't often wear it.

—My father was a Highland dancer. His sisters danced too. Anne sighed.

—I sometimes wonder if we've done the right thing by bringing Dad over here to live with us. But when my mother died we thought –

—He had a sheep farm?

—He lost it in the Depression. He never recovered from losing the farm. He couldn't bear to live in town in a house on a quarter-acre section. He used to stand at the gate, looking out; just looking. Do you think you'll go back to New Zealand?

—I don't know. I don't know.

—Those incessant tea-parties in the afternoon! I couldn't!

Their lives diverged; Grace had never known tea-parties in the afternoon – although there had been one, when she came out of hospital after all those years and someone wrote her a letter, Dear Grace I've read your book. Do you remember me? Will you come to tea with me one afternoon? Yours Katherine. Oh, Katherine! Grace remembered her, a third-former with rosy cheeks and blue eyes. Her father had recently died and she had been surrounded with mists of romance and envy – how wonderful to have a dead father! – and she had begun to write poetry about gardens, and there was a song she sang at the Music Festival,

'There's a beautiful garden by the side of a stream,
where the young people wander and the old people
dream,

171

the flowers ope their leaves like the buds to the light
and close them at evening when dew falls at night.'

In spite of the vague botany, it was, Grace knew, a *lovely* song;
but lovelier was

'To music. Thou holy art in many hours of sadness,
when life's hard toil my spirits have depressed,
hast thou my heart revived with love and gladness
and borne my soul above to realms of rest,
and borne my so-oul to re-alms of rest.'

When Katherine sang that song she was singing of her dead
father, singing in pleasant enjoyment of her bereavement. A
strange girl, Katherine! She left school early to sell buttons
and elastic; she stopped writing poetry.

Therefore, 'Yes, I'll come to tea,' Grace had replied, and
spent a stiffly embarrassed afternoon trying to eat chocolate
cake in a strange house full of tapestries and beautiful furniture; Katherine still cared for things of beauty. Grace said,

—I remember you sang Schubert's *To Music*.

—Did I? I've forgotten. I hated school.

—You sang about the garden, too – 'there's a beautiful
garden by the side of a stream.'

—Oh? We learned so many songs. I was glad to leave
school.

Finding there was no place to unload her memories, Grace
sat quietly trying to eat her chocolate cake; admiring the baby,
the tapestries, the heated greenhouse. Katherine drove her
home, to within a few hundred yards of the house. As she was
saying goodbye Grace could not understand what prompted
her to ask (drowsed, perhaps, in some far-off paradisal image of
childhood, bountiful farms, orchards),

—Would you like a dozen eggs?

She said it suddenly, irrelevantly.

—No thank you, Katherine said, coldly astonished.

They said goodbye, and both promised to meet again, knowing that neither would keep the promise.

———

—I haven't had much experience with tea parties.

—I got so tired of them . . . Aren't Englishmen young? Compared with those at home, I mean. I thought Philip was no more than a schoolboy when I first met him.

—Yes, they're young. It's the sun over there, I suppose.

—Quite likely it's the sun.

(I wonder, Grace thought, if I can lever in a hint that I've had some experience with men?)

—I noticed that about the people in the Spanish islands, Grace said. —The effect of the sun, I mean.

—Oh, you were in the Spanish islands? Did you stay there long?

—Not really. Some months.

(Not yet, Grace said to herself. Almost it's time, but not yet.)

—I suppose you wrote a book when you were there?

—Yes I did a bit of writing. I'm afraid though –

Her heart began to thud, she succeeded in controlling the breathlessness in her voice, and said casually,

—I spent most of the time having an *affaire*. We parted of course. It was interesting though as I haven't had much opportunity to have bed-experience with men.

—Oh I'm sure you enjoyed it!

—Oh yes. Something to talk about when I'm old and in my rocking chair.

There was a collapse of barriers between them; they smiled at each other, secretly, knowingly.

—Well, Anne said in a lighthearted way, —I'd better

prepare dinner. It should be ready by the time Phil comes home from church. We don't want you to miss your train.

—I'll go upstairs to peep at the study.

Before going upstairs Grace went to the sitting room to replace a book. Last night's fire lay dead in the grate. The room was deserted, the empty chairs drawn close to the fire; scattered sheets of Friday's and Saturday's newspaper spoke, as surely as trampled bus tickets on a wet street, of the aftermath of journeys among people. Grace sat in one of the chairs. The door opened softly and Sarah came in with her spoon-angels and her baby Jesus restored to favour. She had come to attend the ceremony which children love but which they have few opportunities to experience – the Private Conference with the Visitor. Sarah sat down, carefully, and put her babies on the chair beside her.

—There's nobody in this room now, she said, emphasising their privacy.

—No.

Both knew that she meant *other* people.

—Mummy and Daddy sit in here at night when we're in bed but there's nobody here now. Do you like my angels?

She held for Grace's inspection the two teaspoons wrapped in their piece of ragged towelling; their oval faces shone where she had polished them.

—I don't know. I think I like them. Are they asleep?

—No, they're awake. They're in bed but they're awake. Baby Jesus is asleep.

—Is he?

—She.

—Sorry, I mean she. Well I meant he but if you say so it's she. She looks fast asleep.

—She is, fast fast asleep . . . Are you going away today?

—Yes, in the train, this afternoon.

174

—Are you coming again to stay with us?

—Well – I – I suppose –

—I want you to come and stay with us again. Will you come to stay with us again?

—Yes, Grace said quickly. Her heart was beating fast with gratitude, love, sympathy, and the extra pleasure provided by a conference ritual carried out by a cunning little strategist, as expert in diplomacy as a General wining and dining with the enemy on a battlefield strewn with corpses.

—Yes, Sarah repeated. —I want you to come here again.

The conference was over. Gravely they went from the room, shutting the door carefully behind them and Sarah, running on ahead to the kitchen glanced back at Grace with that metallic abolishing look which children have when contact has been made, treaties signed.

21

Upstairs in the attic Grace wondered at the nature of those who allow others to enter a room where their deepest secrets lie.

She sat before Philip's huge desk, considering the drawers and pigeonholes crammed with papers and letters and the Imperial Portable typewriter on the desk with a sheet of paper thrust in it, *naked* for all the world to see! Somewhere in one of the drawers perhaps Philip's novel lay typed and bound. How could he dare to give a stranger permission to enter this room! Or was this room not the repository of his secrets? Perhaps he himself had no access to his treasures; perhaps he hoarded them elsewhere without ever recognising them; perhaps he discarded them one by one without ever having known them?

Telling herself that in spite of temptation it is not kind to explore the papers of another whether or not they are admitted secrets, Grace turned her attention to the window which was small, overlooking the golf course and the rigid death-posed trees that stood in their monumental anguish like the thorn trees that are the suicides in hell.

The room, Grace decided, would be a perfect place to write in, although not because of the view, for in writing the studied landscape is not the Holly Road back garden, the Winchley golf course; nor the Old Brompton Road, the car salesroom, the jet cotton-trails in the sky; it is some mysterious place out of the world's depths where the waves are penetrated by the faint gleam of the drowning sun and the last spurts of light escape like tiny sparkling fish into the dark folds and ceaselessly moving draperies of the water; it is the inner sea; you may look from every window in Winchley, London, New Zealand, the World, and never find the Special View. Yet here, in the attic, Grace decided, little effort or encouragement would be needed to draw aside the curtains of the secret window, to smash the glass, enter the View; fearful, hopeful, lonely; disciplining one's breath to meet the demands of the new element; facing again and again the mermaiden's conflict – to go or stay; to return through the window whose one side is a mirror, or inhabit the blood-cave and slowly change from one who gazed at the view to one who is a part or whole of the view itself; and from there (for creation is movement) when all the mirror is a distorted image of oneself, bobbing in the dark waves with stripes of light like silver and gold bars imprisoning one's face and body, to pass beyond the view, beyond oneself to – where? Not to the narrow source that a speck of dust, a full-stop, an insect's foot can block for ever, but to some bountiful coastline with as many waves as beginning fish or sperm before the choice is made, the life decided, and the endowed drop of water shining with its power and pride perfects its lonely hazard under the threat of dust, full-stops, insects' feet; only a multiplicity of wave provides a horizon, a coastline, a land; beyond the view, beyond the narrow vain chosen speck of life to the true source – the boundless billionaire coastline of eternity; from ceaseless rivalries and rhythms and patterns of beginning, to silence and stillness; no wind in the trees – no trees; no sky or people or buildings; to reach there one may need the extreme discipline of breathing: that is, death.

A migratory bird may fly there, Grace thought, and felt

herself immediately there with the touch of airless space upon her feathers; in the skyless world she felt neither leaden nor buoyant; where before in the world the wind curved and ruffled her feathers moulding them into subservience, separating their fronds into trembling fountain-shapes through which the sun, believing them to be the movements of water, hung rainbows; where before the wind guided her flight or sustained her motionless poise, now a surge of nothing enfolded her feathers, as if a cloud were being knitted to enclose her body, yet there were no boundaries; stone-falling, she would fall for ever; the land was for ever.

She longed to return from the source, the speck, the View, to climb through the glass into the attic, and at once, as in dreaming, she was there, with the desk in front of her, the Imperial Portable typewriter (Mine's an Olivetti, she thought. Philip likes Spaghetti Bolognaise; My brother has never been able to eat egg, for years he has never eaten egg), the golf course and trees through the window. She felt cold. She made a last observation of the room – noting in one corner the rucksacks, windjackets, boots waiting to be used for the Highland Holiday. She remembered Philip's words about a visit to the Highlands soon after he and Anne returned to Great Britain.

—We walked everywhere in those days. Remember our first trip up there? You were carrying Sarah at the time, though you didn't know it.

While Philip was speaking Grace had a sensation of walking upon golden stones beneath slow elephantine shapes of cloud trumpeting their light; then suddenly the vast Highland skies had become close, domestic, confined, blue as the best china plate, and Grace felt a movement inside her: Sarah.

In the centre of the attic, piled high, were months and years of literary weeklies and other magazines already brown at the edges, with brown stains on the covers as if Damp (here they talk of him with dread: Damp has got into the house) had come to life and leaned his wet hand upon the paper.

—Now I know where literary weeklies go, Grace thought, with the interest of someone who has solved the problem of flies in winter, pins from a packet, and other such mysteries. A bookshelf near the magazines held Anne's Training College and University books and miscellaneous books belonging to Philip. In this house books had no boundaries; they over-flowed, flooded; you had to stand on the roof waving for help, thinking regretfully of your best cherished furniture already ruined by the rising, seeping ideas . . .

—Are you up there, Grace? There's coffee.

—Oh yes, thank you. Coming!

In the tradition of someone leaving a room Grace gave a 'last lingering look' about her; there was an envelope addressed to Philip; typewritten letters, handwritten letters; suddenly she was aware of his life, his activities, letters coming for him, his reading and answering them. I'm not there, she thought. I'm not there. I'm nowhere. She felt the world go dark with sudden exclusion and she was beating her wings against the door of the dark but no one opened the door; indeed, no one heard.

22

Wait. It was this way, she said. I remember it was this way.

So we were shifting to Oamaru and the shift entailed a longer journey than we had ever known, far more than a few station-puffs in the train, a daylong journey across an endless number of rivers through tussock and cabbage-tree country, moonscape of rabbit warrens overhung with clouds of white dust; railway houses, railway huts, clothes-lines, level crossings in a jangle of warning; sheep, crops; and near Dunedin the dark terrifying lake described to me by Isy as 'bottomless'. We looked out of the window at it; we shuddered, knowing that if we should fall in (how fragile the bridges were across all rivers) we should disappear for ever.

—The Taieri Flats, my mother said, and her voice sounded like doom. A waste of grey mud heaving with buried mammoths which kept moving, surging with lifecurrents over hundreds and millions of years, as easily as small insects and animals flicker with seconds of life after their heart has stopped beating.

Dunedin, and our direction changed, the train seemed to move backwards, we seemed to be travelling the wrong way, going home again to Wyndham. I was sick and I lay with my face against the leather smoke-smelling seat and they covered me with a coat.

—We're going due north now, my mother said, and again

her voice sounded like doom. Why, by saying *due north* instead of *north* could my mother give the impression that the end of the world was near?

Due north. I breathed slowly and deeply at the appalling inescapable reality of it.

—See, kiddies, the Southern Alps!

We looked at the snowy peaks set in an almost unbroken line along the horizon like foam along a sky-sea, and they followed us all the way to Oamaru where they stayed, unmoving now, against the sky beyond Waimate, Weston, Waiareka, and the other places whose names were new to us.

———

In a week we learned to say it, chiefly as a protection against the many strange neighbouring children. It wasn't Ferry Street Wyndham Southland any longer, it was Fifty-six Eden Street, Oamaru, North Otago, our house having a number because there were so many other houses in the street, more than I had ever seen in my life, and rumour said that the street was one of the longest in the town, starting at the seafront, cutting through the main street, gently sloping to our house, past our house, sloping more sharply around the corner to the right, still climbing higher until it reached the Town Belt.

Number Fifty-six was unlike any other house we had ever lived in. It had a bathroom with a bath, a shower, a basin, taps for hot and cold water. It had a lavatory between the wash-house and the coal-shed – a little wooden house with spiders in the corners and a shelf spattered with candle-grease. The electricity which we had never known before provided my father with a new complaining exclamation,

—All the lights in the house blazing! You can see this place all the way down Thames Street; who do you think we are, all the lights in the house blazing?

Thames Street became my father's landmark. If we shouted

we could be heard 'at the foot of Thames Street'; if anything seemingly impossible were demanded the reply came,

—You expect me to traipse down Thames Street!

My father pronounced Thames to rhyme with *lame*. I marvelled at the way he refused, against all opposition, to change it to rhyme with *hem* . . .

So. A house, a garden with a rose arch, a banksia rose summer house where we could act *Hugh Idle and Mr Toil*, two japonica bushes, one Japanese, one red; a plum tree with half the branches hanging over the neighbour's fence; a pear tree with two kinds of pears, honey and winter; apple trees, cookers and Irish peaches; a peach tree which never bore fruit; a fowl-house; a cow-byre; at the back, beyond the garden, the bull paddock, the hill with its caves and fossils, the pine plantations extending for miles; and everywhere, to the left, to the right, across the street, along Glen Street to the gully, so many neighbours and their children . . . the rich people whose children were not allowed to play with any small child who rapped at the door, 'Please c'n Mary come over to play at our place', and the poorer parents who didn't mind where anybody played and who, in the evenings when bedtime was near, stood at the open front doors up and down the street, calling in loud voices, Joh-nny, Joh-nny, the last syllable rising an octave, the word scouring every corner of the insistently sleepless twilight. Our mother, with five names to call, was one of the best callers in the street, with bush Coo-ees added to strengthen her commands which began with the eldest, descending in order of age to the youngest, Isy, Jimm-y, Gra-ace, Dott-ums, Chickabidee! With so many names called there was little likelihood that no one heard, although we tried to establish that only one name had been called,

—Isy, you're wanted.

—Jimmy, you're wanted.

Or, more threatening,

—Dad wants you!

In the end we gave in, wound up our game, said see-you-tomorrow, and trooped home to where our father, tucking into his dinner, would say, with more discrimination than my mother who did not mind (or said she did not mind) who were our playmates as all children of whatever wealth, race, creed should play together,

—I hope you haven't been playing with the Petersen children . . . Don't let me catch you with Billy Walker.

These admonitions thrilled us with pleasure, enabling us the next day to boast, as a condescending prelude to playing with the Petersens or Billy Walker,

—We're not allowed to play with you.

Our piece said, we would enjoy our game, relishing the extra spice of danger provided by associating with forbidden friends. *Associating.* That was the grim word —Don't you let me see you *associating* with Ted McLeod. *Associating* was a more grave crime than *playing with.*

That was Oamaru; everything and everybody swiftly made clear with names and nicknames, nicknames for the admired and friendly, nicknames for the mad, passing slipper-slopper at the end of the street, shaking fists and cursing. The new world was so full of fearful and pleasurable excitements that the movement of them overflowed in me. I blinked, made funny faces, and my mother and father, looking me up in the green-covered 'Doctor's Book' said,

—St Vitus Dance.

—Stop making those faces, my father said. —You've got St Vitus Dance.

—St Vitus Dance, St Vitus Dance!

It was something to tease me with, and teasing-points were

so powerful that we quickly seized them for use one against the other. My nose wobbled like a rabbit's nose.

—I'll put you out in a burrow with the rabbits if you don't stop making those faces. Look at her, just look at her.

My shoulders and arms jerked up and down like pump-handles.

I was six years old, in Standard One at the North School, and it was such a long way to go to school, not a simple 'down the road, across the railway line and around the corner', but through and up and down many streets with choices of this or that street according to time, mood and company. To get home for dinner and back to school in time we had to run and run, jog-trotting with frequent glances at the always visible Town Clock; not to reach the Eden Street corner by a quarter to one meant that all was in vain, we would be *late*. Most of the pupils living up Eden Street had to run at dinner-time and often as I was jog-trotting along, perhaps with the stitch (Oh, I've got the *stitch*), a big boy with bare knees and hairy legs would catch up with me and hiss in my ear as he passed me,

—I'm after you!

And when I sat down to my dinner of mince and potatoes I would say proudly,

—Willy Collins is after me!

Sometimes I put fear in my voice, if I felt the occasion demanded.

—Oh, I can't go down to get the meat and the paper, Willy Collins is after me!

My mother would reply,

—Those big boys have no upbringing.

My mother often talked of 'upbringing'. Whatever it was, we had it.

—I've got upbringing, I said to the girl at school sitting next to me in the single desk. All desks in Standard One were singles, an advance on the primers with their chairs and tables that made you feel you were being put in a doll's house, but how my heart beat fast when I walked by Standard Two's room and saw the double desks which the children talked of as 'jewl' desks. How I longed to sit in a 'jewl' desk! How I longed to be asked to fill the inkwells on Monday mornings! To put the flowers in water and be able to stand, dawdling, alone, out by the taps, listening to the mixed murmur of tables or the singing of *Come Oh Maidens*

'Come Oh Maidens welcome here
you in all the world so dear
come oh maidens welcome here
come oh maidens come,
Gaily our canoe shall glide
row her o'er the flowing tide,
twirling pois shall aid beside
till we reach our home.'

For the teacher to ask me to stay behind to help him after school! To give out the exercise books in the morning!

And how I longed to be able to skip 'Double Dutch' and French skipping alone instead of being 'All in together this fine weather' when the powerful and important children whose mothers gave them *whole clothes-lines* for skipping-ropes would invite the rabble (including me) to crowd into the skip 'for good measure'! Oh the stifling feeling of wonder and admiration when I looked upon the one or two pupils who each season brought skipping 'in'. One day there were no ropes in the playground, the next day a few spun by powerful pioneers; on the third day the excited shout, 'Skipping's in! Skipping's in!'

The days were filled with longings, excitements, discoveries. I discovered geraniums. For days I lived in a dream of geraniums, their name, their colour, the way they spread wild on the banks by the houses in Glen Street. I picked them, touched the petals, crushed the stalks, the juice ran in the cracks of my fingers and hands where my life-line showed, and my heart-line, and my long line of deceit, and, crooked in my little finger, the seven lines which told me the number of children I would have – all my life and my heart and my deceit and my children were drenched with the smell and juice of geraniums!

I skipped to Standard Two, by the window, still not in a 'jewl' desk. The teacher was a young woman who said 'Come out here', and strapped hard, especially on Friday afternoons when we had Silent Reading. One day she looked out of the window and said,

> 'Where the shy-eyed delicate deer come down in a
>   troop to drink
> When the stars are mellow and large at the coming on
>   of the night'

and I sat so still, without making any faces or twitching my shoulders, while the deer were drinking; drink; the brink; link; that was water, lapping, and a quick escape into the forest; the 'mellow' stars; petals, butter.
   —Pay attention!
   Pay!
   —Take out your *Dominion Song Books*!

> 'God of Nay-shons at Thy Feet,
> in the bonds of love we meet,
> Hear our praises we en-treat,
> God defen Dour Free-land.
> Guard Pacifixtrip-lestar
> from the bondsof hate an war

maker praises heardafar,
God defen New Zealand!'

Now *Come Oh Maidens*. Sing up, open your mouths! One,
two. Now *Like to the Tide*.

> 'Like to the tide moaning in grief by the shore,
> mourn I for friends captured and warriors slain,
> here let me weep . . .'

Now sing it in Maori. Come on, open your mouths.

> 'E pare ra . . .'

———

We were poor, there were wage-cuts, talk of the dole; the food
bill went up and up, and my mother put on her best costume
to go down to pacify the rent-man, and suddenly my clothes
were too small and there was no more room for them to be let
out and the Petone aunt sent a dark brown dress smelling of
sweat, an old lady's dress with gathered sleeves and the front
rucked and tucked where old ladies put their titties. The geraniums were dead. And Fluffy the cat was sick. Jimmy was sick
too, in the middle of the night, and my mother ran through
the house in her nightie, crying,
—A convulsion, a convulsion!
saying the middle syllable like a rush of warning, and we got
out of bed, in the middle of the night, as if it were day-time;
yawning, blinking, rubbing our eyes; huddled together with
nowhere to go, no room was safe; the convulsion went rushing
past our ears, like a wind, and no one knew why, no one could
explain.

—Ready, one, two. Open your mouths, sing up!

187

'Like to the tide moaning in grief by the shore
mourn I for friends captured and warriors slain.
Here let me weep . . .'

The sun, shining so brightly in the classroom, was withdrawn. The brown desks and floors and walls with no light to mellow them, turned a dreary colour like furniture in passages where people walk in and out and along, but never stay. A wind coming from under the door clamped cold on my feet in their laceless gymshoes with the holey toes.

Is Grandad dead? Yes, Grandad is dead and he has left behind his spectacles in their velvet purple case, and his pipe, and his razor with the polished black handle.

Fluffy the cat died. I ran round the corner, I could not bear the terrible doom, the chill in the classroom, the song, the lonely beach with the sea sighing in every breath unable to stop or help; and no people, the warriors drowned or slain.

I ran home. Isy sprang out at me with a cry of triumph.

—Fluffy's dead! Look, a Red Admirable Butterfly!

—Dead?

—Poisoned. A Red Admirable. Catch it!

—It's *Admiral.*

—That's the Navy, silly. She's dead. We put her in a sugar-bag and buried her down the garden near the hedge.

But this is Winchley, this is not Oamaru. I am a migratory bird.

23

Grace went down to the kitchen for her coffee. Philip had returned from church and was leaning against the mantelpiece, smoking, drinking coffee, his light-hearted mood apparent in the occasional way he made a grab at Sarah or Noel, flung them on his shoulders or swung them from hand to hand like water-buckets aimed to extinguish the generally still-smouldering mood of Sunday. The kitchen had grown warmer with the meal now cooking and Anne's face was flushed and streaked with red. She sat down, sighing with weariness, at the end of the table to finish her coffee. Sarah, in a sudden rediscovery of the delights of looking from a window, and with the demand that the pleasure be hers alone, was pushing and pinching the tearfully persistent Noel who wanted to share the view although he was not high enough to see.

—Let me see, let me see! was the interpretation of his dribbly moans and wails.

—Sarah, now Sarah! Anne's voice was calm, gentle.

—He wants to look out, Sarah said, with equal placidity, pushing deftly at Noel.

—Let me see, let me!

—Have you read your library book, Sarah?

—I can't find the picnic in it.

—The picnic one's back in the library. This is your new one. Have you read it?

—It's gabbidy, gabbidy, gabbidy, Sarah said vehemently.
—Very gabbidy.

She left the window and went to Philip who pulled her on his knee and sat on one chair with his feet on the other.

—I've been telling Grace about my friend who burps, Anne said.

—Fine. Did you tell her about Wallace?

—Yes, I told her about Wallace and her bedsitter and the cooking.

—Do you always call her by her surname? Grace asked.

—Yes. It's a habit from college days. The roll-call.

Philip turned to Grace. His eyes were like stones with yellow and brown water flowing upon them and flecks of darkness within them.

—In May, he said, —we go to a croft in the far North-West of Scotland where they talk of the rebellion of the forty-five as if it were recent history –

(Oh, not again Philip, Anne was murmuring, smiling.)

—There's Old Dugald –

Philip lifted Sarah from his knee, put down his cup of coffee, stubbed his cigarette in a tray, and stood, facing his audience, to become Old Dugald.

—You should hear him, he said. Changing to a far North-West accent, wagging his arm up and down with his fingers extended, he quavered,

—The Enterrrrprrrise was hopeless from the starrrrt! Aye, Aye!

Everyone laughed appreciatively. Grace remembered that when he interviewed her he had made the same imitation with the same words

—The Enterrrrprrrise was hopeless from the starrrt!

Old Dugald had so struck Philip's imagination that Grace supposed, when he was an old man, baby-bald, his fair skin threaded with veins like ends of scarlet wool, his memories deepened, narrowed, refined, the thought of Old Dugald and

190

the 'hopeless enterrprrise' would remain as a treasure to Philip, a bore to his family or his fellow-inmates at the Old People's Home . . . Grace was frightened, then, at the block vision of time, salt-block, the compression of infancy, manhood, old-age – it was Philip who looked out of Noel's pale peevish snotty little face; she saw Philip glance suddenly at Noel, see himself there, look startled then pleased, then proud. Grace remembered his words in the taxi,

—I'm getting to be a proud parent. The kids are just at the age when they're developing personalities of their own.

She saw his glance of satisfaction at being judged worthy enough to be copied, stamped, re-issued for public scrutiny; also his trembling shock of pride and love as if, staring at Noel, and seeing himself there, he had torn away the neces-sary insulation of the current of life and touched something deadly. Arrested in his *Dugald* imitation (the Enterrrrprise was hopeless from the starrrt!) he looked at Anne; Grace saw him experiencing a different kind of shock – slight, almost pleas-urable; one which caused no injury but which, like the electrified fences used to control wandering animals, per-suaded him to stay within the boundaries of living.

He didn't want to die, he didn't want to die.

Watching him closely, Grace felt his plea, a commonplace human breakfast-plea which changed to a proclamation of Name Rank Number; a sifting and ticketing of his identity; he spoke clearly; there was to be no mistake; he was not this person or that person; name, rank, number; it was clear, wasn't it?

Now the enemy moved in, but there was no capture nor wound, not this time.

—The Enterrprrrise was hopeless frrrom the starrt!

Grace was astonished to realise that the war which began with Philip's chance contemplation of Noel's face had lasted one second or less.

I must be careful, she thought. My mind is spread with a

quick-growing substance, a kind of compost favourable to discarded moments which blossom so tall and suddenly like fairy
trees, and before I can blink my eyes once or twice there's a
forest – birds, animals, people, houses, all sprouted from the
carelessly dropped moment, it is quick and slow motion.
When people say to me,

—What are you thinking?

I see out of the corner of my eye a flash of light; an arrested
flash, a cloud, and stepping from the cloud like kings and
queens from a carriage, the honoured thoughts, attired for the
occasion.

—The North-West Highlands are so like the West Coast of
New Zealand!

Again, again, talking of New Zealand!

—Oh Philip, you *know* how you felt when you were there!

—All the same, I –

Suddenly remembering that he was wearing his best, perhaps his only good suit, Philip began brushing the remains of
children and ashes from his clothes,

—I must change.

When he had gone Grace said, breathlessly

—Oh you are both so wonderful with children! So many
parents – you know – so many parents have no idea how to
manage their children.

(Speaking as if she had much experience with many parents and many children; speaking wisely, in a tone of —I have
studied it, you know.)

Grace was conscious of the relief of moving from the con-
sideration of people to the plane (or 'plain', treeless windswept,
without shelter) of impersonal hints and suggestions for parents;
not as an inhabitant, oh no, merely 'passing through'. She was
up there, waving maxims about like large clean-bladed
windmills when Philip returned dressed again in his checked
shirt and the corduroy pants with the split pocket.

—Oh, he said. —What is this, a woman to woman chat?
Grace looked embarrassed.

—I was saying, she told him nervously, —that you know
how to deal with children – I mean – so many parents – you
know what some parents are like – don't know how to
approach their own children – I mean –

—Treat 'em as furriners, Philip said. —Exactly as furriners.

—Oh no, not exactly, Anne argued.

Grace marvelled at the way Anne dared, without fear, to
contradict her husband.

(No contradictions! Don't you contradict me!)

When Anne said, —Oh not exactly, Grace shivered with
dread, as if she herself were Anne, and yet Anne was not herself but was Grace's mother, oh there was no discipline of
identities, why did people forever exceed their proper boundaries? What terrible theft has there been in my life, Grace
thought, which has removed the power of setting up boundaries, of knowing how to distinguish between person and
person; people are like the sea; I can't be the Dutch boy all my
life, surely!

Grace looked fearfully at Anne and Philip, waiting for the
blow, the shouted, Don't you contradict me, I know what I'm
talking about!

She wanted to run, to hide – in the bedroom, under the
bed, inside the wardrobe.

—Let me tell you I know what I'm talking about. Make no
mistake about that.

—Yes, yes, of course, you're right. 'Blessed are the peace-
makers for they shall be called the children of God.'

Yet listening to her mother and father Grace could not feel
that by agreeing with everything their father said, her mother
was acting as a child of God with a stake in the Resurrection
and first call for being noticed at the Second Coming and
given eternal life. Grace felt ashamed of her mother, she

wanted to go to her and push her, not with words but with her hands, push and hit her; she hated her for being so spineless, and she hated herself for being so much in sympathy; she wanted at last to abolish all confusion of feeling by striking, perhaps killing her.

—Maybe you're right, love. A bit of both treatments, I should say, would be the answer for kids.

Maybe you're right! In Grace's home you *never* admitted that anyone but yourself was right!

—Yes; on the one hand –

They were a text-book couple. Now let's sit down and discuss this like sane human beings.

Grace was suddenly afraid of their seriousness, of the way they *believed*. If she had said,

—I'm a migratory bird. You think I'm Grace Cleave visiting you for the weekend, but in fact I'm a migratory bird; *distance looks my way,*
Philip and Anne would have replied,

—You haven't the outward appearance of a bird. What is the basis for your belief? What proof have you?

It would be useless for her to raise her voice and cry

—I'm a migratory bird, I tell you. I am, I am! Don't contradict me!

They would never answer, —Of course we agree with you, yes yes of course.

That is, not unless they thought her insane.

—I mean, Grace put in, —so many children are treated as if they were babies. All the time. I mean –

Oh who did she think she was, to go talking in this way? Unable to help herself she gave a sudden cry at the thought of having been so bold and foolish, and the cry carried itself by some unexpected trick of air in her throat or perhaps of the feeling in her heart, to her next sentence, making it sound more a lament than a statement,

194

—I'm speaking as one who's strictly outside the circle!

Philip and Anne looked at her, acknowledging that she was outside the circle, then they looked at each other within it, then looked again at Grace who turned to stone thinking There's no fullness, they are scientifically dividing their time, nothing is overflowing.

—Yes, she said, adding to her own horror, —I've studied it . . . well we all have . . . haven't we?

Including them in her knowledge.

She tried not to think of the evening she had arrived to stay; how Sarah had wanted to climb on her knee, and how, when Philip and Anne apologised for the behaviour of their children Grace had said,

—I used to look after babies, you know . . . for years I looked after young children. And of course there was teaching . . .

Teaching? A swollen sickening memory which some day must be lanced, cleaned, reduced to its normal size; an old memory now, it was so many years ago, but it was carried everywhere, free, resembling, though more malignant than, those curious, embarrassing outcrops of flesh which you see on old people usually, inexplicably, on old people getting on or off buses.

Teaching had been a mistake, Grace knew, remembering the Selection Committee from the College and their questions during the Interview,

—What made you decide to take up teaching?

And her false false reply,

—Oh I've always wanted to be a teacher!

(Disregarding the secret diary which recorded – I have told no one, I'm never going to tell anyone, but when I grow up I'm going to be a poet.)

It seemed that she was not grown up yet, nor was she a poet, and if she ever became a poet it was likely that she would never have the *name* poet – it would be '*poetess*', the word which is sprayed like a weedkiller about the person and work of a woman who writes poetry – many have thus been 'put to sleep'; we are assured it is painless, there is no cause to worry then – is there? An absence of pain whether or not it is accompanied by an approved death is a goal to be achieved . . .

—We know where we are, Philip said.

It was a remark of comfort and of warning.

—Yes, time for dinner, if Grace is to catch her train –

—First, Philip said. —Listen. Sit down and listen.

Grace sat where the table had been mysteriously laid for dinner, and while Anne prepared to serve the meal Philip went to the sitting room, and suddenly organ music sounded through the loud-speaker above the kitchen door.

Obediently Grace listened. How could she explain that she preferred to be alone if music were being played? As each note surged within her ear gathering force and resonance like music blown into the secret spiral of a shell, Grace could feel the skin and flesh being gradually removed from her body until only the skeleton

(*What is a skeleton? The bony framework of the body the bony framework of the body*)

remained; then a new force from beyond the music, admitting itself in its perpetual disguise, set to work upon the human bones (the image of bones so familiar and frequent in the human mind – the horrified sympathetic contemplation – I shall be thus, buried, jutting out like a cliff of calcium, gleaming in my phosphorus; a pound of bones please for the dog, marrow-bones; my marrow a mixture of sunflower-coloured lard and mutton-fat . . .) Grace felt her bones changing in material, direction, shape, moulded by the music to one of those metal twists of sculpture set to revolve dancing gleaming in the wind, except that the gallery has forgotten to provide the lifewind; the sculpture is suspended *immobile* but for the occasional influence of heavy human breathing.

196

Grace drew her arms close to her body, hunching them, like thin green metal frog's feet with her hands drooping webbed, in front – bird, frog, woman. Leaning her head on the table she began to cry.

—I'm sorry, I'm sorry. This happens when I hear music.

She controlled her tears; she was trembling.

—How thoughtless of us! Anne exclaimed. — If only you'd told us!

Philip came to the door.

—Like it?

He saw her confusion.

—Turn it off, Philip. It upsets Grace.

—Oh I like it, I like it! Grace assured them. —But I need to be alone to listen to music. I need to be alone!

Suddenly with a wail, bursting into sobs, Sarah ran to her mother.

—Mummy, Grace-Cleave's crying, Grace-Cleave's crying!

Sarah clung sobbing to Anne who took her in her arms, rocking her.

—Sh-shh, it's all right love, Grace is crying because she likes the music.

Philip had gone to the sitting room to switch off the music.

—It's Bach isn't it? Anne said.

—Yes . . . I'm not sure . . . I think so, Grace said.

—Philip will be pleased, Anne said. —We've never had a visitor who's wept.

Recovered, the centre of attention, proud now, ashamed, successful, Grace murmured,

—I'm sorry to make such an exhibition. I do like Bach though.

—I'm afraid I don't seem to be able to appreciate the music Philip plays; it just goes on and on.

—Oh I do like Bach, Grace said quickly, enthusiastically.
—He's, his music's, he's . . .

(She remembered how as a schoolgirl, before she ever heard the music of Bach, she had walked for days listening, listening, in the dream of 'the well-tempered Clavier, the well-tempered Clavier', comforted by the ambiguity of 'well-tempered'.)

Philip came in.

—So you liked our Handel Concerto?

He was smiling at her.

—Handel? I thought it was Bach, Anne said.

Grace made a small sound of agreement, conscious that her prestige was lowered. Perhaps in the best of circles one did not weep at Handel, good old plodding Handel less known for this moving organ concerto than remembered from the Town Hall Days when the combined Male Voice Choir and Women's Institute Choir dressed in their evening clothes to sing the *Messiah*; when the soprano (who later went overseas and was arrested for shoplifting – was it a quarter of a pound of tea or a pair of nylons?) swelled her voice to the plaster-peeling Town Hall roof assuring the citizens of Oamaru that her Redeemer Lived.

Grace sighed. Good old plodding Handel no more. The organ concerto had moved her to tears, her body had been reduced to a metal skeleton mounted in a windless room, peered at and prodded by fee-paying spectators who exclaimed

—The line, the texture, the dimensional interest.

—You say you like Bach? I'm crazy about him.

Philip looked at her, waiting for her reply.

—Yes, I like Bach.

Philip was silent, still looking at her, waiting, in that disconcertingly persistent manner, for Grace to *speak*. Why can't he understand, Grace thought, that all my words are platitudes, that when I juggle and empty out a sentence there's nothing left, no sediment of thought or imagination lies in my speech. Why does Philip wait and wait, like an old peasant at the well, for the bucketful of gold?

—Yes, I like Bach. He's . . . His music's . . . I like him. When I listen to Bach –

It was no use; she could not explain without tripping and falling headlong over clichés, and they were dangerous always, impressing on your mind a stain more deadly because you could not quite identify it, you kept mistaking it for a meaningful spatter of original thought. 'Music of the spheres' indeed! Most music began on earth – in the tradition of the mythmakers who named a definite place of departure to Heaven or Hell; setting out for other worlds you journeyed first to Land's End or North Cape of New Zealand or some spot in Italy, and when you felt the need to return you retraced your steps and were comforted by the sight of familiar land- or sky-marks: rising (or descending) 'we beheld the stars.'

The music of Bach seemed to provide no such place of departure. Earth dissolved; you moved immediately to heaven.

— What were you going to say, Grace? When you listen to Bach –?

—When I listen to Bach, I – I mean – he –

It's no use. I can see it.

His music is a delousing of the spirit, all those little black brain-sucking faith-sucking insects are killed; they shrivel and drop, you can pick them up between finger and thumb, burn them, crush them. Bach's an institutional shower of sound, he's the perfect prison system if you want to know, since we must always pay, sentenced to music. Bach is life-imprisonment with no remission, but what a prison! The routine of a fugue is enough to leave the mind free to hobby ourselves to God. Is God a hobby? You may laugh, Philip, but when I return to London I shall talk to my clergyman about this – the clergyman of my novel.

—You were meaning to say?

—I was saying nothing. I've nothing to say. I'm sorry I cried. It's absurd. Forgive me.

24

The meal was served – Roast Lamb which Philip had shown to Grace on Saturday afternoon, flipping the muslin cover from the plate, thrusting before her the blue-pencilled, censored joint.

—This is your tomorrow's dinner. Genuine down-under fare!

Noel in his high chair, being fed, was grizzling.

—It's his teeth, love. Give him half an aspro.

—Yes, it's his teeth. I noticed one coming.

—The problems of being a parent, Philip exclaimed, addressing Grace.

—Yes, she said knowingly, but it was the clock on the mantelpiece which claimed her attention.

—You'll be all right, Philip said. —We'll leave here in plenty of time to catch the train.

Noting Grace's puzzled expression, Anne said,

—Philip's coming with you, on the bus.

Grace's first thought was

—He wants to escape from the family. The weekend is too much for him.

He seemed to read her thoughts; he laughed, making a joke of the matter,

—Yes, I'll come to the station with you, get away from the howling kids for a while; leave them to Anne. Do you know what Anne's father calls women? The *womenfolk*, he says. He's always advising me,

—Leave that to the *womenfolk*. That kind of job's for the *womenfolk*.

Grace and Anne laughed together. Grace remembered her own father and his insistence that the 'womenfolk' should see to this and that; and underneath Philip's bantering demeanour she sensed a certain measure of relief that there were indeed times when, infected by his father-in-law's attitude he could excuse himself by referring an unpleasant task to the 'womenfolk'. Philip disliked domestic details. Grace recalled that on Saturday morning when Anne had been clearing the ashes from the sitting room fire, and Philip had walked in and, seeing her there bowed before the ashes in the traditional Cinderella pose, had commendably rushed forward with,

— I'll do that, love. Let me do that, love!,
he had appeared relieved when Anne, conditioned to the role of 'womenfolk' urged,

No, No, it's all right thanks,
and he was able, with a mild,

—All right, love,
to withdraw from the scene.

They continued eating in silence broken only by Noel's whimpering. They finished the meal. They were drinking coffee and smoking cigarettes. Dreamily Anne stubbed her cigarette in the melamine coffee-saucer.

—Don't do that, love. It will melt it.

Tense, trembling, Grace looked out of the window, pretending herself into invisibility.

—But I've done it before and the saucer hasn't melted or burned.

—It does, though, with that kind of material.

Anne's voice was calm.

—I'm always stubbing my cigarette like this. It's never harmed the saucer, not as far as I know.

—All right, love.

It was over. Was it? Grace made herself visible once more, ceased her distant gazing from the window, stayed silent, her eyes lowered; waiting, unsure, trapped in her own dread; feeling very much like – an oyster which, believing itself safe, opens its shell, then suddenly sensing danger, snaps within itself, in its haste leaving a part of its body exposed in the shape of a pale fawn pleated frill of dread. Grace could feel herself clamped shut . . . she was home again . . . the everlasting ticket to Fifty-six Eden Street, and it was evening and she was at the state of tiredness where the light from the unshaded electric bulb in the kitchen was a misty pattern of flickering yellow stripes, a hazy waterfall seen through drooping lashes; again and again Grace forced her eyes open and tried not to put her head down on the velvet cushion where the roses painted there by her father dug sharply against the skin; she was waiting, waiting, engaged with dwindling interest and consciousness in the important childhood process of 'staying-up'. Her father had gone 'out the Kakanui' for oysters and her sisters and brother were in bed, and her mother was sitting at the end of the kitchen table patching blueys and a black Italian cloth work-shirt and singing softly to herself the song which she had composed and which was going to earn her enough royalties to pay all the bills and buy a present for everyone – for each of her daughters a 'white fox fur cape'.

—But I don't want a white fox fur cape!

—I'll buy good health for everyone, kind words, a happy home – and a white fox fur cape!

So that was that!

'New Zealand, New Zealand, the land of the fern', she sang, for she couldn't seem to escape from ferns, bellbirds, tuis, kowhai blossoms, the bush – they were a code which everyone understood, which held no surprises, handled and exchanged as currency between Grace's mother and her friends who also wrote verse and composed songs. The bellbirds, the tuis, the kowhai blossoms were always there, like the elves and fairies which their mother tried to persuade them to think about at night instead of being frightened by Dracula, Werewolves, the Phantom of the Opera.

Grace jerked her eyes open. She was trying so hard to concentrate on 'staying-up', to justify the pleas which had earned for her what seemed now more of a penance than a privilege. Soon her father would be home with a sack of oysters which he would spill on to the table; the smell of salt would be so strong that even the bin in the corner where Grace was sitting would seem like a rock in a nest of sea while the waves of sleep, unresisted, lapped and flowed; and Grace would wake up her legs which had gone to sleep, climb from the bin, go to the table and stare at the oysters, sniff the sack-and-salt smell, poke at the few shells adventurously opening and watch them clamp shut leaving part of themselves trapped outside and too scared to open their shell to retrieve it; perhaps it was their tongue which they left exposed, although Grace's big sister had said their eyes were there too, and their ears, that you couldn't really tell with oysters, just as you couldn't tell with snails or with worms whose mouth – she said – was their behind as well, so that when worms opened their mouth you didn't know whether they were speaking or shitting, it was the same thing, not like with people, at least you could always tell, with people.

—Where's the oyster-knife Mum?

A moment of panic; things never stay in their place; oh yes, it's on the shelf in the corner in the scullery. And there it would be, on the shelf, under a dirty tea-towel and a few clothes-pegs, and while Grace was looking at and smelling the oysters and thinking that nothing ever seemed to be gathered by itself from the sea, that what their father had set out to catch, and what he had brought home, could be called a sack of oysters, yet the sea had put in miscellaneous bits of itself – salt, pipis, fanshells, golden and brown weed, grit, sand; all kinds of specimens of the clinging furniture of the sea . . .

Then Grace's father would insert the oyster-knife at a vulnerable part of the shell, force the two halves open, with a quick movement separate the milky-grey oyster from its bed, slide it on to a plate, the oyster-water with it, and offer it to Grace who would tip the edge of the plate (or the shell), drink the oyster-water and suck the slippery oyster into her mouth, shuddering with pleasurable distaste as her teeth sank into the oyster and she realised, too late, that she was eating its *stomach*, probably with giggles inside it; but before she could change her mind and spit it out she had swallowed it, and if she had the shell in her hand she would bite at the small white parking-place where the oyster had begun and had stayed glued and safe.

—

—More coffee? Still dreaming of our Organ Concerto? You know I'm flattered that you appreciate it. So many of our friends sit there dull and stolid.

—Dad hates it. 'Classical' he says. I don't know if you were brought up in this way, Grace, but in our home the wireless was always tuned to the commercial stations and classical music was looked upon with horror.

—Yes, yes, our home was the same, Grace said.

—There. Uncivilised. What did I tell you?

Philip smiled with teasing satisfaction.

—Oh? Grace said. —I didn't know classical music until I was a College student. I had a friend then . . . I had a friend . . .

(I'm not going to tell them, she thought. 'Poor Tom's acold.' There were crocuses in the Octagon, the footpaths were wet with spring rain, and the students, sprawled on the damp grass in Logan Park, were singing,

> 'The Deacon went down,
> O the Deacon went down
> to the cellar to pray.')

—Did you ever learn music?
—Yes. Once. For a time.
(My mother wore gloves to listen to me playing the piano in the front room of a house at the end of a long long path bordered by *aquilegias*.)
Grace glanced uneasily at the clock –
—But I must go . . . I mean . . . I must get ready, but first . . . may I help with the dishes?
—Oh no, oh no. Thanks all the same.

'Getting ready' took no more than five minutes. Grace tried to prolong it by packing and repacking her bag, stripping her bed and folding the blankets as if she had died, turning the pages of the books on the shelf, rearranging the seed potatoes – one had a small brown sprout like a poised horn; looking from the window at the house next door, wondering at the silence, knowing that in the room with the polished window and the widely-drawn curtains there was a tea-trolley in the corner, just inside the door; a clock ticked on the mantelpiece, sturdily, involved in no pathetic fallacies, never confusing its life, like the fabled Grandfather clock, with the beating of the human heart. Oh! Grace smiled, remembering the rude childhood parody,

> 'It was bought on the morn of the day that he was
>   born,
> and was always his treasure and pride!'

Then consulting her watch, deciding that she was 'ready', she went slowly downstairs, lured to the kitchen. She knocked lightly on the door and went in. Anne was washing the dishes, Philip was drying. They were standing side by side, looking at each other, smiling, sharing. Grace wanted to retreat but it was too late. They are complete, she thought. She sat down with a shocked feeling of exclusion. The doors slid silently together and the lips moved, through glass, and she could hear nothing but a slight swish-swish of departure. She almost moved towards them and cried,

—I'm a migratory bird. *Distance looks our way; the godwits vanish towards another summer, and none knows where he will lie down at night,*
but she did not move and she said nothing, and

—So you're ready, they exclaimed, pouring instant hospitality into all the empty pockets and corners, and the room was once again fat with warmth.

Yet Grace repeated to herself, —I've said nothing, I've said nothing. They are used to my silence and stupidity. I've failed, like an automatic machine which is not quite empty but which through a fault in its mechanism can never respond. I wonder what is the fate of those machines choked with sweets, tickets, fortunes, weights, hot chocolate, which are finally abandoned on deserted corners in ghost towns because they have failed to respond?

———

It was as a migratory bird, silent, apart from all human beings, that Grace went with Philip, Anne, Noel and Sarah (together in the pram) to wait for the Relham bus.

In ceremonial procession she and Philip boarded the bus ('we'll go up the front, eh, to get a better view'), and stared through the window at Anne looking so vague and tired that Grace surged now with a guilty consciousness of having herself to herself, preserved, isolated, distributing no gifts night and day to demanding husband, father, children. As the bus passed the forlorn little domestic group Philip waved cheerfully, and Grace waved, a token flutter of her hand up and down. She remembered her fantasies of meeting Anne and Philip – Do have a cocktail! and of herself coping magnificently with conversation ('What wit, what intelligence,' Philip Thirkettle said to his young wife Anne as he donned his silk pyjamas. They were talking of their weekend guest, Grace Cleave, the writer, of limited ability, occasional perception, but in company how dazzling, how articulate: the perfect weekend guest.)

The schoolgirl fantasy depressed Grace. The sight of Anne through the bus window was depressing too   plodding along, pram-wheeling, dowdily dressed, on the far side of the road, being waved to, condescendingly, then turning the corner into the grey gloom of the wintry afternoon with no hope of rescue now whether she walked towards darkness or the fires of heaven or of hell; she could be waylaid by bandits, highwaymen; her husband would not be there to help her, oh no, he was riding with Grace Cleave in the Corporation Bus to Relham.

—You've another book coming out soon?

—Yes, in summer. It's hopeless. And there are some stories.

—You've had some in the *New Yorker*?

—Yes. I've been living on the proceeds for the last year. They pay – they pay a huge sum, quite out of proportion –

She could see that Philip was waiting for her to name the sum, but she was shy of doing so – how could she explain that she had been ashamed and embarrassed (pleased too) at being paid so much for a few hours' work when a complete book was rewarded by a tiny spurt of royalties as useful as toothpaste forced from the end of an almost empty tube.

—Yes, out of all proportion.

The bus stopped. Conductor and driver were going off duty. Grace smiled to herself as she thought of the London buses and their individual exasperating behaviour – of the buses behind schedule which sped recklessly along when one had set out to make a leisurely journey, of the buses ahead of schedule which dawdled and finally stopped in quiet streets when one was in a hurry; of the drivers and conductors who went off duty and were not replaced; how an urgently summoned inspector arrived to call to the restless passengers,

—Everybody off and on to the bus behind!

Trampling, shuffling, having tickets endorsed; complaining, complaining –

—Strange things happen in London, Grace confided, —when the driver and conductor leave the bus.

She was used to making wild statements which were not questioned but were taken for granted, therefore she was startled and confused when Philip, alert, sensing that at last she might have some interesting, intelligent, imaginative communication, turned eagerly to her,

—What happens?

Grace felt a surge of despair. It was true that in her life she had converted conversation for her own ends, that when she spoke to anyone it was less from a desire to communicate an observation or idea than from a personal need to allay her own fears. She was so unused to conversation in the accepted sense that most of her spoken words were almost meaningless. They were a gesture, like that of a hostess arranging loose covers on the furniture of her room in order to assure herself that everything was prepared for her guests. Grace worked so much with words that her prostitution of them made her ashamed and depressed – but were they not so *convenient* a way of saying nothing, of sounding, without inviting too much ridicule or enmity, a self-confident bleating of one's identity, which, put forth at the appropriate time and place could even be disguised to resemble a *fanfare of importance?*

—Well?

This is Northern obstinacy, Grace felt, as she sensed Philip's determined waiting for her reply.

—Oh, nothing happens . . . I mean, not much. The driver and conductor get off the bus and don't return and the bus is stranded.

—I see, Philip said politely in a tone of disappointment.

I don't really care for the front of the bus, Grace thought angrily as she felt the shuddering engines and the throbbing warmth and moved her feet in the cramped space, resting them against the sloping floor as if she were in a shoe-shop trying on shoes.

—It's an observation hardly worth making, she said.

—Oh I don't know, I don't know, Philip said.

—But mysterious things do happen.

For a moment he looked concerned.

—Of course.

They walked towards the station. (You needn't come, really; I can find the station and the train.) Philip noted, identified the architecture. Wearily Grace said

—Yes, yes.

—I'm not boring you with all this? You *are* interested?

—Oh yes, yes.

Yes: an ugly shorn affirmative; prison treatment for ideas crowding behind the bars.

25

On the station platform.

—Like something to read?

—No, no thank you.

With sudden gaiety Philip laughed aloud,

—See? I promised you wouldn't miss the train!

She was used to being laughed at for arriving early for appointments, trains, buses. She prided herself on her habit as a personal possession which she had earned and paid for; it was at least some means of proclaiming herself to the world

—Oh I'm always early for everything. I'm *fearfully* early!

She enjoyed Philip's laughter. His swift expression of gaiety had reached her and touched her, had retrieved a part of her which she could not offer in speech (yes and no having so few pockets); his laughter had been like one of those instruments like extended arms which shopkeepers use to reach, clasp, and bring within bargaining distance, the packets of dusty old-fashioned goods placed on remote high shelves.

They walked along the platform.

—You won't want to go in an open carriage?

—Yes, I do.

He looked puzzled, almost annoyed, as if her choice of a closed carriage should have been inevitable. (Hadn't she said, —I don't go to places where there are many people, not to concert halls, crowded theatres . . .?)

—Very well.

He was disappointed. He liked consistency.

He found her a corner seat facing the engine, and he stood long enough to satisfy his conscience that he had delivered her to a seat worthy and safe for travelling, then he disengaged himself – it was a physical act, like the falling away of the outer casing of a rocket as soon as the rocket enters another stage of its journey into space. She felt suddenly alone, unprotected.

—You will come again, anytime, no need to give warning?

—Yes I will.

—Bye-Bye.

The absurd farewell irritated her; she could never grow used to the English 'Bye-Bye' spoken with such seriousness by grown men and women.

—Goodbye, she said firmly.

He was gone then. She did not wave from the carriage window, but leaned over in her seat, pretending to pick up something from the floor, and when she sat upright again he had left the platform. Quickly she got up, hurried to the lavatory, defied all rules about 'only when the train is in motion', returned to her seat, unfastened the ribbon of the chocolate box which Anne had filled with chocolate coconut-sprinkled squares, and began to eat. By the time she had eaten the top layer the train was moving from Relham. She replaced the lid on the box, retied the ribbon, and was about to lean back to doze when she realised that the upholstery seemed more luxurious than usual, also that there were few passengers in the carriage. Suspiciously, anxiously, Grace addressed a man sitting at the opposite window.

—Excuse me, this is a *Second Class* carriage isn't it?

The man looked up from his Sunday newspaper.

—Yes, he said.

With a sense of relief out of all proportion to the occasion, Grace sighed.

—Thank goodness, she said. —For a moment, just for a moment I thought it was *First Class*.

She dozed. The train moved through blizzards; coke fires glowed through the haze of powdery flakes; the landscape, all ugliness concealed, was smooth and soft as a pillow. Once, opening her eyes with a start, Grace thought she saw blood on the snow, but it was only the shadow of the burning braziers.

The little stations passed in quick gulps, then all was smooth and secret and Grace saw nothing through the window but the carriage lights and her own reflection. Then the train jerked, swung from side to side, leapt across an unseen gulf, slowed down, dragging its burden towards London.

———

Grace inhaled the smoky stuffy atmosphere of her flat, frowned at the one letter, an electric light bill, lying on the carpet, switched everything on – lights, hot water, fires; bathed, extravagant, lonely; prepared her typewriter and papers for the next day's work, flipped through the unfinished typescript, shuddered at her inability to compose one beautiful dignified sentence; and, trying to establish in her mind the events of the next day, the day after, the day after, which would make living endurable, and finding it difficult to think of any events beyond food, the possible completion of one perfect sentence, the once-weekly visit to the psychiatrist,

(—I went away for the weekend. I'm a migratory bird), she crept between the sheets of her innersprung First Class bed, headboard extra, and slept, turning sometimes and moaning, seeing Noel, Sarah, Philip, Anne – Anne saying —I thought I'd get some sheeting, I thought I'd get some Parmesan; and then flying to Philip's wild wet West Coast, 'The Enterrrprrise was hopeless from the start', then home, Cheerio

Mum and Dad, in the white stone city, Fifty-six Eden Street, with flies in the room and flypapers hanging from the ceiling, and flies, swarms of frantic buzzing flies in Grace's hair; and then panic, First Class or Second Class? – but does it matter, for *Distance looks our way; the godwits vanish towards another summer and none knows where he will lie down at night.*

Acknowledgements

Many thanks are due to the following: Harriet Allan and the whole team at Random House New Zealand for their painstaking care over this project; Jane Parkin and Claire Gummer for their editing skills; the English Department of the University of Otago for practical assistance; Michelle Bennie for making the digital transcription; the Community Trust of Otago for a grant to the Janet Frame Literary Trust enabling background research to be undertaken in archive collections; curators at the Hocken Library, Dunedin, NZ, the Alexander Turnbull Library, Wellington, NZ, and Pennsylvania State University Special Collections Library, USA, for their cooperation; June and Wilson Gordon for their encouragement; Charles Brasch's literary executor Alan Roddick, for kindly approving Janet Frame's use of the Charles Brasch poem 'The Islands' as a central theme for this novel; the Janet Frame Estate's literary agent Andrew Wylie and the staff of The Wylie Agency for their expert handling of the sale of English language and foreign rights; Lawrence and Marion Jones for wise advice and moral support.

My deepest gratitude goes to my fellow Board members Denis Harold and Lawrence Jones for sharing the responsibility for the decision to offer this manuscript for publication. Janet Frame entrusted the care of her literary estate and charitable trust to us, but left no specific instructions about *Towards Another Summer*. She made it clear that it was too personal to publish in her lifetime, but since she bound two copies of the typescript and preserved them in separate locations, and made no secret of the novel's existence, we have concluded that she anticipated posthumous publication. Thanks also to Denis and Lawrence for helping to set protocols and oversee the copy edit and proof correction process.

Pamela Gordon
Chair
Janet Frame Literary Trust

Every effort has been made to identify and contact copyright holders of quoted material; the publishers and the Janet Frame Literary Trust would be grateful to hear from any copyright holders of material that we may have inadvertently missed. Acknowledgement is made to the following for kind permission to reproduce the listed extracts:

Charles Brasch, extracts from 'The Islands' (epigraph, pages 58 and 59), 'Waianakarua' (page 48) and 'A View of Rangitoto' (page 58), reproduced by kind permission of the Estate of Charles Brasch; the words from 'The Islands' on pages 206 and 213 have been reordered by Janet Frame.

Allen Curnow, extracts from 'Time' (pages 40 and 55) and 'Landfall in Unknown Seas' (pages 135, 137 and 157), reproduced with kind permission of Jenifer Curnow, Auckland.

John Masefield, extract from 'Tewkesbury Road' (page 186), reproduced by kind permission of The Society of Authors as the Literary Representative of the Estate of John Masefield.

C.K. Stead, extract from 'Pictures in a Gallery Undersea' (page 140), reproduced by kind permission of C.K. Stead.